Eden felt his s

And it was how she imagined it would feel when a star collapsed in on itself in some giant, epic implosion. She knew without even needing to open her eyes that he had seen the box of spare tests, so she opened them anyway because choosing not to see something didn't stop it from happening.

Harris was holding one of the boxes in his hand. His beautiful carved face looked like a bronze Emesa battle mask, and she felt her ribs snap tight as his gray gaze locked on to hers. She knew that she had gone pale and that there was no way to hide that.

"You can't be pregnant. We used a condom."

There was a short, stifling silence as his gaze switched to the other boxes on the counter, then back to her face.

"Are you pregnant?" he said hoarsely.

Ruthless Rivals

Let the billion-dollar battle commence...

The feud between billionaire CEOs Tiger McIntyre and Harris Carver is legendary. Once, the determined and outrageously handsome duo were a force to be reckoned with. Until a perceived betrayal put an abrupt end to their friendship and ignited a ferocious rivalry... They just never expected it to put them in the paths of the only women with the power to take them—and their *hearts*—down for good!

When Tiger discovers his new assistant is actually a hacker working for the enemy, he uses the unfortunate situation to his advantage. By demanding that Sydney's next act is being his fake date in Venice!

Boss's Plus-One Demand

After his attempt to bring down his rival backfired spectacularly, Harris needs to do some damage control. Only, his new PR manager, Eden, is the woman he spent one passion-filled night with! And she's carrying a scandalous surprise...

Nine-Month Contract

Both available now!

NINE-MONTH CONTRACT

LOUISE FULLER

Harlequin
PRESENTS

Harlequin®
PRESENTS™

ISBN-13: 978-1-335-93971-5

Nine-Month Contract

Copyright © 2025 by Louise Fuller

Harlequin Enterprises ULC
22 Adelaide St. West, 41st Floor
Toronto, Ontario M5H 4E3, Canada
www.Harlequin.com

Printed in Lithuania

MIX
Paper | Supporting responsible forestry
FSC® C021394
www.fsc.org

Louise Fuller was a tomboy who hated pink and always wanted to be the prince—not the princess! Now she enjoys creating heroines who aren't pretty pushovers but are strong, believable women. Before writing for Harlequin, she studied literature and philosophy at university, then worked as a reporter on her local newspaper. She lives in Royal Tunbridge Wells with her impossibly handsome husband, Patrick, and their six children.

Books by Louise Fuller

Harlequin Presents

The Italian's Runaway Cinderella
Maid for the Greek's Ring
Their Dubai Marriage Makeover
Returning for His Ruthless Revenge
Her Diamond Deal with the CEO

Hot Winter Escapes

One Forbidden Night in Paradise

Behind the Billionaire's Doors...

Undone in the Billionaire's Castle

The Diamond Club

Reclaimed with a Ring

Ruthless Rivals

Boss's Plus-One Demand

Visit the Author Profile page
at Harlequin.com for more titles.

CHAPTER ONE

HARRIS CARVER STARED down at his phone, his stomach clenching around a knot of frustration and disbelief. The voice message from Sydney Truitt, the hacker he'd employed to find his intellectual property on Tiger McIntyre's server, was short and to the point.

'Sorry. *I failed.*'

Her voice sounded as tense as he felt but then she had just waved goodbye to a life-changing amount of money. But that had been the deal. No IP, no fee.

His IP. The schematics for a drill bit that Tiger had stolen from him to make his own prototype. He felt his shoulders and spine tense, his frustration giving way to an old, familiar anger that accompanied any mention of his greatest rival.

Tiger McIntyre.

They could have been allies. They had been best friends at university.

Growing up with half-siblings who had both their parents on site, he'd always felt like an inconvenience, a burden. An outsider. But he and Tiger had the same interests, the same determination to succeed. They'd been like brothers.

Or so he'd thought until he'd caught Tiger with *his* girlfriend.

He'd been nineteen, raw with jealousy, drunk on the pain of their betrayal, so of course he'd hit him. Tiger wasn't called Tiger for no reason so naturally he'd hit Harris back and the whole thing had escalated. The dean had got involved, and Tiger had kicked off again and then been kicked out.

Since then, everything they had planned had come true. They were business rivals now and like two apex predators they circled one another, keeping their distance but always aware of the other's movements. That had been bearable until Tiger stole from him. He always had people keeping a close eye on his biggest rivals and the drill-bit prototype sounded near identical.

His hand tightened around the phone. He had been livid, a mindless fury that blunted all reason or calm. On some pretext of wanting to upgrade his security systems, he had got his people to reach out to a hacker: Sydney.

But in reality, he was looking for revenge. Sydney, or rather her feckless brothers, needed money and so he'd offered her a temptingly large enough sum to hack Tiger's system and find his IP.

He'd planned to ruin Tiger by revealing the theft but now he had nothing. No proof. No means of revenge.

Outside, a quarter moon seemed to sneer down at him, and he stared at it furiously, reminded as always of his father's blank, uncomprehending face when he looked at Harris. As if he were talking to a stranger rather than his son.

At the time, his degree and subsequent career path hadn't felt like a conscious choice, but he could admit now, to himself at least, that it had been partly driven by a hope that it would bring him closer to his astronaut father.

It hadn't.

His father had been interested in the science and the engineering but not proud or happy that his son had chosen to follow obliquely in his footsteps.

He stared across the room at where the rain was running down the windows. It made him feel as if he were drowning and, abruptly, he got to his feet.

What he needed was to get out of this apartment, out of Manhattan and go find a woman who, like him, was looking to lose herself in the white heat of an anonymous one-night stand.

It took ten minutes for him to pull on some jeans and a T-shirt and a battered leather jacket that he'd loved the hell out of five years ago right before his business had taken off into the big time.

He caught the subway downtown. By the time he emerged back at street level the rain had slowed to a light drizzle. As he slipped out of the side entrance to his building, he started walking. He had no idea where he was going but it felt good striding down the sidewalk without the shadow of his security detail. It would mean a ticking-off later, but he was the boss and, for what he had in mind, two was company, anything more would be a crowd. Besides, the risks of anyone recognising him were low. It wasn't as if he were a movie star.

Not that he didn't get his fair share of female attention.

More than fair, he thought, as he sidestepped past a couple of women who both glanced over at him in unison like synchronised swimmers, their eyes narrowing approvingly, mouths curving into smiles that made his pulse beat harder.

They were beautiful, but it was too easy, he thought as he carried on walking. What he wanted was friction. Something that would chafe and burn a little, just enough to give him something to focus on other than the pain and frustration in his chest.

His footsteps faltered.

In the weeks that followed he would wonder what made him stop.

From the outside, the bar wasn't promising. Or visible, in fact. The door was down a flight of stairs and there was no name above it, which was why he had almost walked straight past. But then he'd heard it, a faint but steady bassline pulsing in time to his heartbeat.

He doubled back and ran lightly down the stairs. As he pulled open the door, the sound and heat hit him like a wall.

The bar was rammed.

At one end of the room a hen party wearing sashes and devil horns were shrieking and giggling around one of those old-fashioned jukeboxes. There was a huge TV screen on the other side of the bar, and a large group of mostly men were gazing up at the two boxers slugging it out. Of course, it was the heavyweight title fight tonight. No wonder it was so packed in here.

It was perfect. All of it. The noise, the smell of hot, excited bodies and cheap alcohol, and, best of all, nobody knew him. Here in this downtown bar without a name, there were no pasts or futures, just a present filled with possibility.

He hesitated for a moment and then he joined the

swaying, sweaty throng of people waiting for a drink. At this point in his life, that was a novelty. He couldn't remember the last time he'd waited for anything. When you were as rich as he was, there was never any waiting. Doors opened; tables magically un-booked themselves. There was always a car or a jet on standby.

'Excuse me—'

He moved aside automatically to let the woman pass, his brain carrying out a silent but thorough inventory. Petite. Brunette. Smokey eyeshadow and nude-coloured lips. Small, heeled boots and a sleeveless floral dress that made him think of the last days of summer, and last, but registering loudly in his mind, a tiny tattoo on her shoulder of an apple with a bite taken out.

She turned. 'So, what do you want to drink?'

Her voice was light and husky and at first he didn't realise she was talking to him. He was too busy trying to place her accent—she was American but there was a hint of something else, English maybe?

But then he felt the pull of her gaze, and the pounding music seemed to skip a beat as their eyes connected.

Hers were green and narrowed like a cat's, and impatient, he realised with a jolt as his gaze snagged on her soft pink mouth or, more specifically, on that kissable, full lower lip, which was curved up questioningly in his direction.

He felt it jerk him forward like a fisherman's hook. *You*, he thought, *I want you*. His pulse was vibrating violently, and his breath felt hot and dry as if his chest were a furnace. His first thought was outrage that she could do this to him, and so effortlessly. And he almost wanted to punish her for making him feel so out of control and unlike himself.

Only wasn't that exactly who he wanted to be tonight?

Yes. But in his head, he'd thought it would be more transactional. More you scratch my itch and I'll scratch yours. Sex as a balm. An analgesic to soothe the chaos inside his head. But this woman was already kicking up sparks and overturning tables.

He cleared his throat. 'You want to buy me a drink?'

She shrugged. 'You look thirsty, and I'll get served before you do so I thought I'd offer but if you're happy to wait—'

Good luck with that, he thought as she ducked under his arm. She only came up to his shoulder so the chances of her attracting the barman's attention were zero whereas he—

'A San Alvaro. And a shot of Coughlan.'

She didn't raise her voice, but he felt the huskiness in all the right places. The barman seemed to as well, stopping in his tracks as if he'd been shot with a stun gun.

The woman glanced back at him. 'Last chance.'

His fingers twitched as something charged shimmered in the air between them.

'I'll have what you're having,' he said.

She rocked back on her heels, that green gaze skimming over him assessingly—critically, he realised. And that was not so much a novelty as it was a challenge.

'Make that two of those.' She had turned back to the bar, and he took the opportunity to admire the mass of dark silky hair that clung damply to her shoulders. And to imagine what she would look like wearing nothing but those boots.

His skin felt hot and taut and, blanking his mind, he shifted his stance. 'Are you celebrating?'

Her face stilled a fraction. 'No, I just need to cut loose.'

From what? Or who? As if he had spoken those questions out loud, she turned. Her mouth pursed in a way that made him lose his bearings momentarily, as if it were him who had been cut loose.

'It's been one of those weeks, you know?'

He did. Rarely had things gone so off-piste for him. 'Will next week be better?'

She seemed surprised by the question or his interest, and he was surprised too because he wanted to hear her answer. Wanted to keep her talking.

'Yes.' She nodded, but there was a vulnerable slant to her gaze that pulled at something inside him because he understood the need to hide weakness or doubt.

'Let me get them.' He leaned forward but she was already holding out her phone to pay.

'It's done.' Her eyes met his and he felt the challenge there like a lick of flame. 'Here.' She handed him the bottle and the shot glass. She had small, slim fingers and her hair wasn't uniformly dark but threaded through with reds and golds. Her skin was gold too and so smooth it looked as if it had been poured over those curving cheekbones.

'Then let me get the next round,' he said, his body moving closer to her of its own accord.

Her lips parted to show small, white even teeth and she stared at him for a moment, her chin tilted up. 'You don't need to do that. I'm not keeping a tally.'

'Maybe you should.'

Her eyes were very green then and his pulse jumped for no reason as she held his gaze.

'Fine, I'll keep a tally and when I've made up my mind what I want, I'll let you know,' she said in that husky way of hers that made his body feel loose and restless and yet tenser than he had ever felt.

'See you around,' she said abruptly and before he could respond, she had melted into the crowd. After a moment, he shrugged mentally and made his way over to the group of men gazing up at the screen.

An hour later he was still gazing at it. He liked sport, but his mind wasn't really on the match. It was stuck, like a stylus skipping in a groove, endlessly replaying that moment when the petite brunette with the dare in her green eyes had spun on her heels and left him standing there.

See you around, she'd said. But where was around? His eyes scanned the bar again as they'd been doing roughly every five minutes since she'd walked away from him.

But there was no sign of her.

His fingers tightened around the bottle. He could have settled for another woman. More than half a dozen had brushed against him as they'd walked past. Others had stood nearby with their friends, laughing in that way women did when they wanted you to look at them.

Only he didn't want what they were offering. Without his permission, everything inside him seemed to be interested in just one woman.

One of the boxers, the reigning champion, lunged forward, and there was a roar of approval from the spectators as the contender stumbled backwards. Watching the boxer crumple, he felt a surge of animalistic satisfaction, gratification almost, but it wasn't enough.

And then he felt it.

Cool, concentrated, intent. Seeking him out. A tractor beam, except they didn't exist outside science fiction. No, this was like the gravitational pull of the moon on the sea. Or perhaps it wasn't, he thought as he turned around. Perhaps it was something that had less to do with physics and more to do with biology.

She was standing by the door, her green eyes fixed on his face. Not just standing. She was watching. Waiting. For him.

He felt suddenly untethered. Unbalanced.

Earlier, he'd thought he wanted a distraction. Not any more. Now he wanted to focus. On her. To feel her body against his, beneath his. He wanted the frenzy and release that touching her, kissing her, possessing her, would bring.

His breath floundered in his throat, hot and heavy like the blood stumbling in his veins, and the noise in the room faded as it all gave way to the pounding of his heart.

For a moment, he couldn't move, and then he was shouldering his way through the crowd, stopping just far enough away from her to make it impossible for him to give into that wild, nearly ungovernable urge to pull her against his body and take what he wanted from her mouth.

'I've made up my mind,' she said slowly, and there was a hoarseness to her voice that he felt everywhere. 'I know what I want now.'

His mouth was suddenly dry. She was talking about a

drink, obviously. Except that he knew she wasn't. Only he needed to hear her say it.

He met her eyes. 'Same as before?'

For a moment, she didn't reply, and he felt a flicker of panic that he had misunderstood, but then she took a step backwards and pushed open the door.

'Let's get a room.'

It was an invitation or a dare. Maybe both. Either way it didn't matter, because the answer was yes, and, heart thudding against his ribs, he reached for her hand.

Eden felt the floor shudder sideways beneath her feet as he took her hand. His fingers were warm, his grip firm and the calloused skin on the palm made her blood race through her limbs as they left the bar.

Outside it was raining hard. People were running for the subway, sidestepping puddles and clinging to their hoods. But she barely registered it.

Since walking into the bar earlier, she had barely registered anything.

Except him.

She had noticed him straight off. Wanted him too. Who wouldn't?

He looked older than her, early thirties maybe, and he was tall and broad and blond. Not the Nordic kind of blond. His hair was the colour of ripe wheat and early morning sunlight and the palest acacia honey.

But it wasn't just his blondness or his height or the breadth of his shoulders. He had been scanning the bar, and there was something about his intense concentration and his stillness and the latent power beneath that stillness which reminded her of some gorgeous, sleek predator.

Because obviously, he was also immoderately and shockingly gorgeous.

His face was a masterclass in scale and symmetry. And there was something about the shape of his skull.

She wasn't an artist, but she had watched her mother and grandmother sketch and paint most days and she knew what beautiful bone structure looked like. And this man had beautiful bones. *Beautiful everything*, she thought. He turned to look at her, his slate-coloured eyes fixing on her face as he pulled her underneath a shop awning, pressing her body up against his and fitting his mouth to hers.

Her belly clenched as he parted her lips and deepened the kiss and it stunned her, the rawness of his desire, his hunger. And hers.

It was hot and mindless, and she forgot they were in the street and that it was raining and she didn't know his name because, whatever it was he was doing with his mouth and hands, it felt as if he was claiming her. Reminding her that she was his.

He drew back and stared down at her for so long she couldn't breathe. And then he took her hand and began leading her back the way they had come.

She felt a rush of panic. Had he changed his mind? Her fingers tightened around his, pulling down hard—

He stopped and turned.

'What are you doing?' she asked.

He frowned. 'I need to go to the drugstore. I don't have any condoms.'

'That's fine. I have some.' She opened her purse and their eyes met as she thrust one into his hand.

'There's a hotel back there on the corner. I saw it when

I walked by. They might have a room,' he said finally and the hunger in his voice made her breath go shallow.

She stared at him, shivers of anticipation dancing over her skin. She had walked into the bar to get out of the storm. But there was a storm in his eyes that she wanted to hurl herself into.

It had been such a difficult week, and it was a good thing that people saw only the face she chose to present to the world. None of the emotion she was feeling had been visible, which was lucky because inside everything had been a howl of chaos. Like a tornado in a jar. They had made one once at school and for a short while she had been fascinated and excited by the power she'd had to turn the still, clear liquid into a swirling maelstrom.

Only it felt different when someone else held that power in their hands. A power to turn your life upside down. What made it worse was that she was supposed to be over Liam. And she was. Even if he offered her the moon, she wouldn't take him back, but there was a part that felt connected to him still. To what they'd had.

What she had lost.

He shouldn't have texted her.

She shouldn't have read the text. Or looked at the accompanying photo. Had he no heart?

Stupid question, she thought, remembering Liam's handsome face and the confident gaze that had seemed to rest on her so approvingly back then. He had no heart. He was like the Tin Man, except he didn't want to change. Which was why he could send a photo of his new baby to the woman he'd lied to. The woman who had loved him and miscarried his child shortly before he'd broken up with her.

It was too late for regrets. Except apparently it wasn't, so for days now, she had been teetering on a ledge, swamped by a need that she couldn't control.

Her eyes moved to the man staring down at her.

But he could.

He could quiet this chaos beneath her skin.

She reached up and touched his shirt, too scared to touch his skin in case it lit the touchpaper beneath hers, but still needing to feel him.

'Yes,' she said, and he took her hand and they started to run.

The hotel did have rooms. The receptionist on the front desk seemed unfazed by their lack of luggage but then this was New York in the fall. Probably loved-up couples were constantly tumbling through the doors like autumn leaves.

Not that they were in love. This was purely about sex and that was exactly what she needed it to be about.

She watched as he pressed the keycard against the lock, on the door to their room. *Their* room.

As if *they* were a couple.

The weird thing was that it did feel as if they were. The moment their eyes had met back in the bar; it had felt as though he could see through her armour. See past the small, taunting smile and the glitter of her green eyes. It felt as if he saw her, knew her. Or maybe it was that he wanted to know her, know everything about her, and she had a sudden, ludicrous urge to lay out all her secrets before him.

Even just thinking that might happen should have sent her running back down the stairs and through the hotel foyer and out into the street because she had never felt this way. Normally, she was clear in the moment. Her motives were simple. It was just sex for the sake of pleasure and to feed that human need for intimacy in bite-sized portions.

Her hand moved to touch the apple on her shoulder.

A bite, that was what she wanted, all she could contemplate.

But this felt different.

'Have you changed your mind?' His voice snapped her thoughts in two and she turned to look up at him. In the half-light of the hallway, his beauty should have been lost to her, but it wasn't. If anything, the shadows seemed to highlight the flawless contours of his face.

'No.' She shook her head, and he pushed open the door for her to step into the room.

It was small but clean with just three pieces of furniture. A mirrored dressing table, a chair and a bed. But that was all they needed.

She heard the door close, and turned to face him. For a moment or three, they just stared at one another. Then he took a step forward, his arm sliding smoothly round her waist, and, tipping her face up to his, he kissed her.

It was like the Fourth of July.

She moaned against his mouth, her hunger for him beating hard in her blood. His taste was making her dizzy. Nothing to do with the whisky. She could taste his need for her, and it was intoxicating. He felt incredible. Hard and smooth, and she wanted to feel more. He clearly did too because his hands were moving over her urgently, taking a path that was as tortuous as it was potent.

Shivery pleasure danced across her skin, and she

arched helplessly against his body, her hips meeting his, nipples hardening as they grazed his chest.

She began pulling at the waist of his jeans, clumsily, her fingers urgent but ineffectual, and he made a noise in his throat. Wrenching his mouth away, he yanked his T-shirt over his head, then unbuttoned his jeans and pushed them down his thighs in one smooth movement.

There was a beat of silence, pure and stunned like a ray of moonlight hitting glass.

She felt her face still, knew that he must be able to see her reaction and tried to turn her head to compensate, but she couldn't look away. She didn't want to because he looked even better than he felt.

Heat, liquid and electric with currents that moved in sharp, expansive ripples, was pooling between her legs, and she could feel a pulse leaping erratically in the hollow on the left side of her throat.

Better was an understatement.

She breathed out unsteadily, her gaze pulling with magnetic force to where the thick swell of his erection was pressing against the fabric of his boxer briefs, and then her heartbeat shuddered sideways as he tugged them down too, letting them fall to the floor.

Yes.

Yes.

Yes.

The word blinked inside her head three times like the lights on a fruit machine. *Jackpot.*

He was definitely a prize, she thought, stepping forward and running her hands over his chest, drunk on the feel of the hard, smooth muscles. And for one night only, he was hers.

All of him, every glorious, *naked* inch.

She licked her lips.

He had the most incredible body. It made her feel… Actually she had no idea how to describe what she was feeling, but it wasn't just his body. It was the way he was looking at her. The intensity of his eyes.

'I want to see you naked,' he said hoarsely, his breath hot against her mouth, his fingers pulling at the buttons of her dress. Which was what she wanted too, and yet—

Her body gave a silent yowl of protest as she pulled back. 'No, not like this. I want you to watch me undress.'

His pupils flared and a muscle jumped in his jaw. *Better*, she thought. She wanted him to watch, to wait, to want her as much as she wanted him.

He stared at her in silence as she stepped backwards, small, slow, steady steps, *impressively steady*, she thought, given that she knew how it felt to have his mouth and body fitted against hers.

It felt as if his dark grey gaze had already stripped her naked. His expression was hard and unfathomable but his eyes, they were molten heat, and she felt a corresponding heat bloom low in her pelvis.

Head spinning, she pulled at the buttons of her dress, feeling his gaze, his intense focus and the flutter of the fabric against her bare thighs as it slithered to the floor.

He said nothing, did nothing, just stared at her, but that muscle was pulsing in his jaw again and there was a dark flush along his cheekbones that made her belly clench.

No one had ever made her feel like this, helpless and out of her comfort zone but also hungry and strong and demanding. It was so confusing, without precedent, but it felt right, she felt right. With him, she was the woman she wanted to be, the woman she had lost somewhere along the way.

Her fingers reached behind her back to unhook her bra and that soon joined her dress. Now he moved, walking slowly but purposefully towards her, his eyes not leaving hers, all smoke and shadow, so that it felt as though they were puncturing her skin, and yet it also didn't feel real. It was as if she were dreaming…

He stopped in front of her.

'I've got it from here,' he said then and she jolted back to him, feeling the authority in his voice like flames licking her body. His mouth found hers again, his hands were on her waist, and his body was hot and hard against her. Blood roared in her ears, and she felt her belly flip as he lifted her hair away from her neck and kissed a path down her throat, then lower to the swell of her breasts. His lips closed around first one, then the other nipple and she arched against him, lost in the sensation of his open mouth and his tongue and his warm breath and the heat of his body.

He moved closer again, close enough for her to feel the insistent press of his erection against her stomach, and she felt an answering wetness between her thighs.

As if he could feel it too, one hand slid down her body, over the curve of her waist, and her breath fluttered in her throat as his fingers pushed under the waistband of her panties, inching down—

They stilled and she almost cried out in her frustration and then he moved his hand to part her thighs, pushing gently into the slick heat. His thumb grazed the hardened bud of her clitoris and she leaned into him blindly, her mouth seeking his, her hand reaching for the thick length of his erection to steady herself.

Her fingers tightened infinitesimally around him. He felt amazing. Hard and solid, with a life force that beat through the palm of her hand in time to the stampeding of her heart.

He grunted, and she felt his breath catch and then he was gently batting her hand away and rolling a condom on. She gasped as he pulled down her panties and then spun her round so that she was facing away from him, towards the mirror.

The blood roared in her ears as she stared at their reflections.

His eyes were dark like hammered pewter. 'It's your turn to watch,' he whispered against her throat. 'Touch yourself, baby.' He nudged her fingers towards the triangle of curls between her thighs, his hand covering hers as she did what he asked, his other hand clutching her hip, pressing the curve of her bottom against his groin. Dazedly she pushed backwards. He felt so hard and with every passing second she was softening, becoming liquid, turning inside out, her whole body expanding, shrinking and tightening around an ache that she could taste in her mouth, a need that only he could satisfy.

He was nipping her throat, not biting, just letting his teeth graze the soft skin, watching her intently as if she were the most fascinating thing he'd ever seen and that almost sent her over the edge.

'Wait,' he said in that way of his that was both commanding and soothing. 'Just a little longer. Let it build.'

He touched her breasts, pulling gently on the nipples,

and she gripped the dressing table, whimpering, wanting more.

'Now—' she said hoarsely. 'I need you now.'

She felt the change in him as his control snapped. He parted her legs and then suddenly he was thrusting into her, moving rhythmically, his body lifting and rocking her like a strong current at sea, his hand gripping her shoulder, his fingers stroking her clitoris so that she wanted to climb out of her skin and fuse with his.

A noise rose in her chest, involuntary, burning her throat as it burst from her lips. She writhed closer, desperate for him as something hot and wet and impatient swelled inside her, humming and quivering and stretching and contracting and—

The jolt of pleasure hit her with such force that for a moment it was impossible to do anything but hang there tautly, straining, outside her body and yet so much a part of his that she could feel his heart thundering beneath her ribs.

And then it burst inside her, leaving her breathless and panting and stunned. This was more than pleasure, it was sublimation and she let it roll through her as he jerked against her, his big body thrusting upwards. Now she was being pulled out on his tide, buffeted by his waves, rising and dropping back down again and again and again and again.

Eden woke in the darkness to a car alarm. Thinking it was a different type of alarm, she reached for her phone only to realise her mistake. For a cluster of seconds she had no idea where she was or how she had got there. But then she sensed the man sleeping beside her and she remembered everything.

Every glorious second.

She pressed her hand against her mouth to stifle the moan that rose to her lips, to stifle the hunger that seemed almost ill-mannered after her greed earlier. And also, to stop herself from reaching out and waking him. She couldn't ask for more, and not because it would be rude to do so but because if she let herself touch him, she honestly didn't know if she would be able to stop.

She couldn't go there again. She couldn't ever allow herself to need someone like that, not even for sex. Not after what happened with Liam. Her chest tightened around the imperfectly healed wound beneath her ribs. Even though things had ended between them so long ago, it had been such a shock to find out that he was a father. Despite the small screen on her phone, she'd been able to see the likeness between him and the baby. He had looked happy, and she knew it made her a smaller person, but she'd hated him for that.

Hated that he now had what she'd unknowingly lost.

Hated him for proving to her that she was not genetically programmed for intimacy and permanence.

Which was why she wasn't going to wake him now. This beautiful stranger who had opened her up with his soft mouth, bored into her with his hard gaze and even harder body. His touch had been so urgent, so precise, and powerful, possessive and devastating. Staring into the darkness, she could still feel the imprint of his hands on her belly, her hips and between her thighs.

She stared down at him, watching his chest rise and fall, trying to memorise the details of him—the curve of his jaw, those ridiculously long eyelashes, the contoured muscles of his arm—wanting to remember everything, to hold on to him for as long as she could in her mind at least.

Surely that was allowed.

But then how did she know?

She had been raised by her mother and grandmother, two single moms with big hearts and bad taste in men. The kind who weren't looking for love or anything like it. They would be there for a couple of days or weeks, maybe even months, but then they left because, '*You can't catch what don't want to be caught.*' That was what her grandma used to say when her mother was weeping on the porch again, watching the tail lights of yet another car disappearing down the street.

Growing up, watching from the sidelines, she had been sure in the way that children could be about things they didn't fully understand that the stable, loving, respectful relationships that had eluded her mother and grandmother would not be out of reach to her.

She had been wrong. Because now she knew love was a game that you couldn't win unless you knew the rules. Which she didn't.

But now she had new rules. Better rules.

Liam's betrayal coupled with the heartbreaking loss of her baby weren't things she could survive again. Better to face reality, which was that Fennell women didn't attract the kind of men who wanted marriage or long-term relationships or exclusivity.

These days intimacy for Eden meant sex, not love and certainly not marriage, and as far as settling down went, well, she had an office space in London and had

just opened up another in New York and she was building a roster of wealthy, international clients who kept
her constantly moving around the globe. Plus, she had
an arrangement for regular short term lets in the same
apart hotels, which felt like a kind of semi-permanence.

Truthfully it was all she could manage. A deeper commitment would simply highlight the lack of it elsewhere
in her life. And it was enough for her.

Or it had been until last night.

She had never suspected that two bodies fusing together could produce such fire. Or such honesty. Of
course, he hadn't known that she was opening herself to
him not just physically, but emotionally, releasing all the
confusion and tension and turmoil of the last few days.

That was what she'd done, but only because there was
this barrier of anonymity between them. Now, though,
she had to leave. Because it felt as though she had given
away too much of herself and the last time that had happened, her world had turned to dust.

She dressed quietly and forced herself to leave without looking back.

Downstairs, she approached the concierge's desk. It
was a different receptionist, which made it slightly easier
to do what she needed to rebuild the barriers she had let
fall, and then she was pushing open the doors and stepping into the cool dawn air.

Outside the roads were silent. It had stopped raining,
but the sky was a mottled purple, streaked with gold like
the cover of one of her mom's old glam-rock albums.

Normally, she liked waking at dawn. At home, her
mom and grandma almost never closed the curtains, and
she found the serenity of those hours comfortingly fa-

miliar. But not today. For some reason, the first pale rays of sunlight that were creeping down the buildings made everything feel abandoned and desolate.

She felt abandoned and desolate, which was ridiculous because she had abandoned him. Her nameless lover. Picturing him on the bed, his head in the crook of his arm, she felt a pang under her ribs that was so intense and sharp that she had to reach out and steady herself against a lamp post.

He was a stranger. She didn't even know his name. He didn't know hers either, but he'd touched her as if he knew her. As if she were his. And she had wanted to be his. Wanted to burn in the wildfire he had unleashed.

Her heart was banging inside her chest. It made no sense for her to feel like this.

It was just sex. Only she'd had 'just sex' before and it hadn't felt like that. Before, with other men, it had been instant gratification and been as instantly forgotten. And last night should have been no different.

But even though she would never see him again, she knew she wouldn't forget him.

Don't think about it. Don't think about him, she told herself. *Just do what you always do. Don't look back. Just keep moving—*

It had started to rain again, and she felt a pang of relief, and something like regret. But if that wasn't a sign to keep moving, she didn't know what was, and, flicking up the collar of her jacket, she began to walk quickly down the street, keeping her gaze focused on the cracks in the sidewalk.

CHAPTER TWO

THERE WAS A cracking sound like a bone breaking as a Y-shaped branch of light flickered across the bruise-coloured sky above New York. The fierce storms that had been predicted by weather forecasters all week had hit the city that afternoon.

But nature's most powerful pyrotechnic display was like a damp squib in comparison to the tension in the HCI boardroom.

Lounging back in his chair, Harris scanned the faces of the people sitting around the table, a slight narrowing of his eyes the only sign that he was even listening to the debate taking place.

'Enough.'

He spoke softly, because he could. Because everyone in the room was paid to listen to him. Then again, they would still listen even if no money were involved. Wealth was not a prerequisite of leadership.

It was one of the few things his father had taught him and maybe that was why he had always remembered it, because evidence of the father-son bond they nominally shared was scant and mostly negative.

But that had stuck, and so he had trained himself to speak with intention and conviction, to always be prepared and to get to the point. And not to shout. Speaking calmly and quietly made people stop and listen and being heard gave you power.

His father had taught him that as well. His mother too. Growing up, he had felt neither seen nor heard.

Or wanted?

His spine stiffened against the leather upholstery, and he pushed the question away, reluctant to even acknowledge it within the privacy of his head. The past was unassailable. Fixed. It was history. There was no point in wasting time and energy on it. What mattered was the present and here he was respected, and for good reason. He had built a business from the ground up and he was taking it to the stars. Metaphorically and literally.

HCI was currently in the process of finessing a remote AI-powered lunar module, which, if things went according to plan, would be searching for minerals on the moon's surface roughly this time next year.

Unfortunately, due to his impetuous and ill-judged attempt to expose Tiger McIntyre, things were no longer going to plan. Not only was his reputation under scrutiny but his shareholders were rattled. Enough for him to call his C suite into the boardroom for this unscheduled meeting.

There was no direct evidence linking him personally to the hacking of Tiger's server and plenty of people would think it was just one billionaire throwing shade at another, but shareholders hated conflict and scandal.

The irony was that he hated it too, but Tiger pressed all his buttons. Which was why he'd gone and hired Sydney and it had seemed to make perfect sense at the time. Tiger was known to cut corners and blur lines. All he'd had to do was prove it. The idea that he would end up in the firing line simply hadn't ever occurred to him.

'This is getting us nowhere.'

A drumroll of frustration, irritation too, because he wasn't the bad guy here, vibrated against his ribs as he stared down at his laptop, his eyes fixing on the headline that played on his name: *What a Carve-Up!*

It had started small. Just a couple of carefully worded paragraphs about rumours of IP theft and industrial espionage on a blog online.

Naturally, he hadn't been named as the perpetrator, but his was a niche industry. There were only so many people it could be. Then again, the Internet was a rumour mill. Surely no rational person would be swayed by something so random and half-baked and, having run it past his legal team and his head of Comms, he had taken their advice and decided to simply ignore it. To do otherwise would be to give it credence, to fan the flames that would shrivel and die of their own accord if deprived of the oxygen of publicity.

And that was what had happened. Everything had gone quiet.

Job done. Problem solved.

Until today at five o'clock, Eastern Standard Time, when everything had come crashing down around his ears.

Because of course it wasn't just any blog. The Bit Bucket might have started out as a nervy, acerbic column by MIT dropout, Chase Fordham, but it was now the go-to destination for anyone looking to take the pulse of big business.

In other words, those two paragraphs were actually a

baited hook. And someone had taken the bait. A much bigger fish, big enough to name names.

His name.

He scrolled slowly down the two-page article in the *New York Chronicle*. It was good journalism. Punchy, and unfortunately true. Deniably so, but the damage was done.

Which was why he was here in the boardroom instead of heading off to Monaco to look at his latest yacht. Another twinge of irritation.

Stifling it, he glanced up, the pen in his hand tapping out a clear message to the people sitting round the table even before he spoke. 'I'm struggling to understand what it is that I'm looking at.'

Outside the storm was raging but nobody inside the room was watching the clashing clouds and flashing thunderbolts.

They were watching their boss.

'Isn't this story supposed to be dead?' He spun the laptop round to face the table. 'Because from where I'm sitting, it appears to be not just alive but in excellent health.'

His lawyer cleared his throat. 'Obviously, the source is anonymous, but we have our people looking into—'

'I am way past worrying about who the source is,' he said firmly. Obviously, his team knew nothing about his ill-advised meeting with that hacker but even if she hadn't signed an NDA, he knew this 'leak' had nothing to do with Sydney Truitt. This was Tiger McIntyre. It had his paw prints all over it. 'I want this story shut down.'

'And we can do that, sir,' his head of Comms, Avery Williams, said. 'But if we want to deny it—'

'I do,' he said coolly.

She nodded. 'Then first off, we need to issue a statement denying any allegations of wrongdoing. And then we need to focus on reminding everyone exactly who you are and what you stand for. We need to set the record straight and give you the opportunity to be the man the world thinks you are.'

Her words echoed inside his head. She made it sound so simple and in theory it was. He had a reputation as a meticulous, straight-talking, cool-headed businessman that was fully justified. Except when it came to Tiger. Even hearing his name made him feel awash with a rage that he knew was both excessive and irrational.

A rage that had momentarily blocked out all logic and good sense so that he had momentarily 'gone rogue', acting on impulse, driven by a need to take down the man who had so casually betrayed his trust and treated their friendship as something disposable.

It had been an uncharacteristic act of recklessness, and the worst part was that he still hadn't managed to punish Tiger. Instead, he was the one being made to jump through hoops.

Lifting an eyebrow, he stared steadily at Avery. 'And how exactly are you planning to do that?'

She hesitated. 'I know you like to handle most media matters in house but, on this occasion, I think it would be better to involve a reputation management agency with specialised experience in mitigating these kinds of negative incidents.'

He nodded. 'So, you want to start interviewing people?'

Avery smiled at him. 'I've already hired someone. All you have to do is meet them.'

* * *

Avery's words were still echoing inside his head as he took one of the nutritionally balanced meals from the fridge at his triplex penthouse that his chef prepared every day and dropped down onto one of his huge cream-coloured sofas. It was still raining heavily, and he stared out of the window at the blurred New York skyline, mechanically forking up edamame beans and smashed avocado.

His body still felt so on edge, and he could feel the tension humming beneath his skin as if the storm were trapped there. It was Tiger's fault he was feeling like this.

And he hated him for it. Not that he could hate him any more than he already did, and that would never change.

But other things were going to have to, he thought irritably. Unlike Tiger, he was not of the opinion that all publicity was good publicity. His PR people worked hard to keep his name out of the headlines so that he could ensure that his life ran like clockwork. Now, though, he was going to have to do whatever it was people in his situation did when they messed up.

He tossed his half-empty plate onto the sofa, his hand moving automatically to reach for his wallet.

Gazing down at the photos in his hand, he leaned forward greedily.

The one on top was an ultrasound scan. It looked like one of those weather maps on TV of an incoming storm, all indecipherable curves and lines at first. Then your eyes adjusted, and you could detect the shape of a baby lying on her back, her nose distinct, arm waving up as if to say, here I am.

Now he held the two photos side by side and looked at the second.

After nine months in the warm, watery gloom of the womb, his newborn daughter's small face was scrunched up against the light, grey eyes, *his eyes*, wide and still stunned after the shock of birth, her tiny, flawless fingers curled like petals against some kind of shawl. She had been perfect. Unreal. Miraculous. Only he hadn't realised the miracle of her until after she was born and was living on the other side of the world from him.

By then it was too late. She was gone.

He'd found her again, but it had taken years and money that he didn't have back then. By the time he'd been able to pay someone to find her so much had changed. Jasmine had a new father. Not new to her, because he was the only one she'd ever known. Which meant that Harris was not only absent but superfluous as well.

Obviously, he had a legitimate biological claim and these days he had unlimited wealth with which to demand his paternal rights. Only it wasn't that simple. He knew from personal experience that after food, shelter, warmth and comfort, what every child needed was stability and him barging back into her life all these years later felt like self-indulgence, not a right.

He flinched as a snap of lightning illuminated the room, momentarily blinded, just as he had been earlier when the photographers had swarmed towards him. He'd been lucky today. The tumultuous weather had been on his side, but it wasn't going to rain for ever. The press would come back and in greater force. So, as much as he wanted to pretend this wasn't happening, that wasn't going to work.

Decisions and actions, both had consequences. He was still living with his from twelve years ago. He stared down at the photo, his heart swelling to fill his chest.

It had been taken in the hospital just after Jasmine was born. Taken by the man who had stepped up in his place. A man, not a boy.

That's what Jessie had needed when she'd told him she was pregnant.

They'd done the paternity test and he'd been supposed to go with her for the scan but had bottled it. He'd been so young and hadn't been ready to be a father. Hadn't been in love with Jessie. And his parents' marriage had shown him what happened when you forced people into a lifetime commitment under those exact same circumstances.

So he'd made a bad choice, never thinking that it would have such absolute and irreversible consequences.

But it had.

He hadn't understood it at the time but that one small decision had been the last straw for Jessie.

She'd needed a man who was willing to support her, not a teenager hoping it was all a bad dream and that he was going to wake up real soon.

That was why he'd skipped the scan. He'd done the paternity test, but the scan would make it scarily real. When he hadn't shown up, Jessie had reacted accordingly. Within days she was gone, back to Australia and out of his life. Had he realised that would happen? Had he understood the full, lifelong consequences of that moment of panic and cowardice? Had he imagined another man becoming Jasmine's father so quickly? No, he hadn't.

But even if he had, would he have done anything differently? Would he have fought to change Jessie's mind or tried to make it work between them? Probably not, because deep down a part of him had thought she'd be better off with someone less damaged. Someone who could be the father his daughter deserved.

That was part of his reasoning then, swimming in the slipstream of his panic and shock, the need to not repeat the mistakes his parents had made. They'd been two square pegs forced into a round hole because he'd been conceived by accident. Was it any wonder their marriage had failed? And failure came with fallout.

They'd remarried other people and had more children. Half-siblings, who, through no fault of their own, were a constant reminder that he was on the outside. They were the focus of their parents' love and attention, and he was always an afterthought, a reminder for ever of a past everyone wanted to forget. A visitor who stayed in the guest bedroom.

His beautiful daughter must never experience the pendulum swing of two homes, because it was a lie. In reality, two homes meant no home. Just a temporary address with a pull-out bed surrounded by boxes of books and old sports equipment, and an angry, confused boy lumped in with all the other unwanted, unnecessary detritus of life.

He breathed out shakily. Thankfully, he could afford to give his daughter an entire suite of rooms, decorated just as she wanted. Money was no object.

His shoulders tensed. It was an empty phrase and also misleading because money was just an object, a thing. But it also had the power to change lives and it would be disingenuous to pretend that his money didn't matter to him or other people.

And yet, it had limitations. Jasmine lived in a world where she felt safe and seen. He had hired a very expensive investigator to make discreet inquiries and she'd reported that his daughter was happy and stable, so his money could only offer her material things. Better things? Possibly, and more of them. But did that really matter? Arguing that it did made him feel shallow and he didn't believe it anyway.

This whole Tiger McIntyre mess was doing his head in. To get it sorted, he needed to be the man the world thought he was, but right now he just wanted to lose sight of that man. To break free of him. To be a stranger to himself.

What he needed was a distraction. Could he call Rebecca?

They had ended things two months ago. Not because he didn't like her. He did. She was smart, driven and beautiful, but she had started dropping the odd hint about the future. Their future.

That wasn't what he wanted. Not now, maybe not ever. Or maybe it wasn't about wanting or not wanting it, but instead not knowing how it worked.

As a kid, he'd always been fascinated with the inner workings of machinery. That was another thing he and his father had in common, that need to open up the hood and see the mechanism, to understand the nuts and bolts, the cogs, the pistons.

That need to know was the engine of his success.

But he didn't know how to make a relationship work. How could he when he'd only ever seen them failing?

He got to his feet and stared out at the city below. The rain had stopped again and at street level the lights flashed as they changed colour, beckoning him as they had the other night.

Heart throbbing against his ribs, he watched them blink, red then green—

Green eyes and a tattoo of a bitten apple on her shoulder.

A pulse of heat beat across his skin as he replayed what had happened when he'd met her two weeks ago.

His hand splayed against the glass as he scanned the city skyline.

Who was she? And where was she now?

If only he could snap his fingers and summon her here.

If only...

'Excuse me, Mr Carver.'

Harris looked up at his PA and frowned. 'What is it, Sean?'

'Ms Williams just called. She sends her apologies but says she's going to be another fifteen minutes.'

Fifteen minutes was nothing in the scheme of things, but he didn't like waiting at the best of times, and this was far from the best of times. But that's what this meeting with the reputation manager was all about. Putting the worst behind him and regaining control of his narrative.

Then, finally, things would go back to normal.

Tapping his fingers on the armrest, he stared around the room. He could have had this meeting at the office, but he preferred using the club for anything more sensitive.

The last meeting he'd had here was with Sydney Truitt. Same room, same chairs. The difference was he'd been on his own and that should have been a red flag because he should have had his people there. Except he hadn't been able to because what he'd done was funda-mentally, legally wrong. Not that there was any hard evidence to connect him with the rumours. His lawyers had been very clear about that.

Unfortunately, there was always that lingering sense of no smoke without fire. Rumours could and did do enormous damage.

It was too late for regrets, though. Yes, if he'd told his team what he was planning the meeting would never have taken place. But he'd been so furious with Tiger, he would have ignored every flag including the skull and crossbones.

And the rest, as they said, was history.

Or rather he'd like it to be. Currently it was very much in the present, but, shutting down the memory of what had been far from his finest hour, he glanced at his watch. 'Fifteen minutes, you say?'

'Yes, sir. But the reputation manager is already here. Would you prefer to wait for Ms Williams? I can take some coffee—'

'No, send her in. Let's keep things moving. Ms Williams can join us when she gets here.'

As was usual with an outside hire, he'd been sent a short biography and résumé of the person, which ordinarily he would have read.

Ordinarily.

But for some reason, he'd barely skimmed the report. He couldn't seem to concentrate. His mind had been all over the place.

Instead, time and time again he had thought about that hotel off Bowery.

His eyes narrowed as if he had X-ray vision and could see through brick and plaster into the hotel room where he had spent six hours at most.

Six hours. It wasn't even the length of a working day, but if he closed his eyes, he could replay almost every minute right up until the moment he fell asleep.

Then the screen went blank.

Because she'd left without waking him. Without saying goodbye or leaving so much as a note. Oh, but she had paid for the room.

He knew he should open his laptop and read the report through quickly, but his gaze kept being pulled towards the windows. The staff hadn't closed the drapes and something about the arrangement of the fabric nudged forward a memory of waking alone in that hotel room. Feeling alone, and wronged. As if something had been stolen from him.

He'd hated that feeling.

He gritted his teeth. Hated too that she had paid for the room. He knew that it was ridiculous, but he did.

But why? No doubt she earned a wage so why shouldn't she pay for the room?

And yet, still it rankled.

Which was no doubt why his brain remained so fixated on her.

Now, though, he needed to focus on the matter at hand. He picked through his memory for anything he could remember about this woman from the conversation he'd had with Avery when she'd told him they'd found someone.

'*She's a bit of a wild card,*' Avery had said. '*Not in ability. She comes highly recommended, even though Ale-*

theia One is a small agency. She's just opened a second office in New York, but she started out as a one-woman band. She's young and very media savvy and there's a creativity and a freshness in her thinking that I think could work very well for us.'

We'll see, he thought. This interview was a formality really, a nod to his authority and an opportunity for him to meet the successful candidate, but he was always wary about outside hires. They might lack loyalty, and this IP theft accusation was such a sensitive issue.

Of course, his team had done everything by the book. No details of what had happened would have been released until the NDA was signed. And yet, despite that caution, Avery had still hired someone who was, in her own words, a 'bit of a wild card'.

He heard the door open.

'Mr Carver. This is Eden Fennell.'

He felt it first in the air.

A shift of something, a tightening, so that momentarily he was distracted enough to get to his feet on autopilot, holding out his hand to the woman standing in front of him.

And then his brain caught up with what his eyes were seeing, and he froze.

Petite. Brunette. No smokey eyeshadow this time and the tattoo on her shoulder was just a blur beneath the sleeve of her cream silk blouse, but the green eyes were the same and once again they were narrowed on his face.

It was the woman from the bar.

And this time she had a name.

Eden.

CHAPTER THREE

EDEN STARED UP at the man standing in front of her, her
fingers clamped around the handle of her purse, her heartbeat silenced, shock and disbelief flooding her veins. And
then a shiver that had nothing to do with shock or disbelief scampered over her skin because it was him. It was
the guy from the bar.

Only in some ways seeing him again shouldn't have
been a shock. For the last couple of weeks, she had been
thinking about him continuously. And not just thinking.
She had found herself looking for him too.

And she had finally found him. Or maybe he had
found her?

Waking that morning in the hotel, she had greedily
watched him sleep, wanting, needing to remember him.
But now he was here and the sheer randomness and im-
possibility of that was making her feel as if she were
floating outside her body. She almost reached out to grip
his arm to see if he was real. Behind her, she was aware
of his PA's slightly stunned gaze, probably because nobody in history had left his boss standing there with his
arm frozen in mid-air, but she couldn't move or speak.

Harris Carver recovered first.

'Ms Fennell. Thank you for meeting me,' he said, his voice sending a hard shiver down her spine.

I wasn't meeting you, she wanted to say. I was supposed to be meeting a billionaire CEO with a reputational crisis.

She knew the name, of course, and him by reputation or should that be reputations? Because he had two now. The first was low-key and immaculate, a bit like that expensive suit he was wearing.

Her eyes flicked over the dark fabric. Sleek lapels, trouser hems hitting the tops of his shoes, the jacket moulding to those broad shoulders and chest. Subtle details that elevated what were essentially the by-products of sheep and silkworms into the perfect example of quietly luxurious amour for a business titan who preferred to stay out of the limelight.

A frontrunner in the field of space exploration, Harris Carver was known to be hardworking, detail-driven and discreet. He never spoke out of turn, never made waves, except in the financial markets where shares in his company kept rising as if they too wanted to reach the stars.

In other words, he was not supposed to be potential client material for her.

But that had all changed a couple of days ago.

Now he was being linked, not openly, but the clues were there, to claims of IP theft and industrial espionage; only the brief she had been given was so carefully worded it was impossible to identify him as the client.

And even when she'd signed the NDA, she still hadn't connected his name with the man who had unravelled her so completely.

Beneath her feet, the floor started to shake as she felt the memory of that night swirl inside her, warm and dark and honeyed. But she couldn't leave him standing there any longer and, stiffening her shoulders, she reached out and shook his hand. 'Mr Carver.'

His grip was warm, and firm, and she could feel the hard calluses on his fingers. It was all too easy to remember them sliding over her naked belly as he stared down at her with hot, hungry eyes...

She felt his hand tighten around hers and her breath jerked in her throat as she met his gaze head-on. There was nothing warm in his eyes now. Instead, there was a cool anger and the fading aftershocks of a surprise that made no sense because, unlike her, he must have known who he was going to meet today.

She knew how these things worked. His people would have given him some kind of synopsis of her career to date, and all the pertinent facts would be accompanied by a photo. Which meant that either he hadn't been curious enough about who he'd hired to check them out or he hadn't recognised her from the other night.

Given his earlier reputation as a meticulous, detail-driven workaholic, the former seemed unlikely. But thinking that she had slipped his mind stung. Not that she would ever admit that to anyone, him most of all.

She pulled her hand loose. Working as a reputation manager at this level had taught her a lot about herself. She knew she was resilient. Smart. Adaptable and ambitious. But it had also taught her a lot about wealthy, powerful people. What she'd learned was that showing weakness was a taboo.

And they didn't get much more wealthy or powerful than this man.

'I think we'll take that coffee after all, Sean,' he said, but his eyes stayed on her because it was simply an excuse to get his PA out of the room, she realised a moment later, her stomach somersaulting as Sean retreated. She heard the door click behind him. Harris Carver did too because his pupils swelled, the black eclipsing the grey of his irises, and she felt the effects of it stampede through her body.

They were alone.

The air stretched around them and, for a fraction of a second, she thought he was going to lean forward and fit his mouth to hers as he had done in the street.

But this was reality, not some fantasy.

He took a step towards her. 'What is this? What are you doing here?' The tension in his voice rippled through her.

She frowned. 'You know what I'm doing here. You hired me.'

He shook his head. 'Right, so I'm supposed to believe that this is all just one big coincidence, you and me in that bar and now you here.'

Her eyes clashed with his. 'Is that a question?'

'I'm asking you if that was a coincidence?'

His voice was all serrated-edge consonants and clipped vowels. Did he think she had somehow engineered their hook-up? That she'd slept with him because she thought it might give her an edge over her rivals?

No, that was ridiculous. He couldn't think that. For starters, the timings were all wrong, and, anyway, his people had reached out to her.

'I don't go hunting for clients in bars, if that's what you're implying. Sorry to dent your ego but I didn't recognise you that night, and it's not as if we exchanged names and contact details.'

When you worked with a high-profile, high-net-worth individual, discretion was mandatory. Potential clients often used a go-between in the first instance who would outline a 'theoretical' reputation crisis event and request a strategy, but client anonymity was common practice up until an NDA was signed. Today was no exception.

Sure, Harris Carver's name had been in the news over the last few days, but he was one of a number of notable people currently facing down a reputational crisis. And as she'd just told him, she'd had no idea who he was that night.

She did now.

It was still making her head spin that this man and the man who had been stalking through her dreams every night were the same person.

Her pulse twitched as she thought back to the moment they'd met. He'd been wearing jeans and a T-shirt and that battered leather jacket and she'd *assumed* he was just an ordinary guy meeting up with mates to watch the big fight. And when he'd taken her hand, his skin hadn't been smooth and soft like the hands of some pampered billionaire. She'd *assumed* he was a mechanic or a carpenter.

Wrong assumptions.

'And that's my fault?' His voice was an explosive mix of anger and frustration, and he was staring at her as if she were an intruder he'd caught opening his safe.

Which was not only deeply unnerving but unjust.

'It's not mine. None of this is my fault. I didn't even

get told who I was meeting today until your PA came and got me. But you knew who I was. If you had a problem with that, why didn't you—'

'I'm so sorry I'm late.'

They both turned as a middle-aged woman in a pale grey trouser suit hurried into the room, accompanied by the PA carrying a tray of coffee.

'There was an accident out on—'

'It's fine, Avery.' Harris Carver cut across her explanation. 'We've literally just started.'

He turned back to Eden, his expression flat and unreadable. 'Ms Fennell, this is my head of Comms, Avery Williams. You have her to thank for your being here today. She championed you from the start.'

In other words, had he played a part in the selection process, he wouldn't have chosen her, she thought. But he didn't have to say it out loud. The taut twist to his mouth did that for him.

She held out her hand to the head of Comms. 'It's lovely to meet you, Ms Williams.'

The older woman smiled as they shook hands. 'So, where are we up to? Obviously, you've been introduced.'

Eden nodded. 'I was just saying how surprised I was that Mr Carver agreed to hire me given what he knew about me.'

The other woman's face froze momentarily. 'Why? Have you met before?'

'No.'

They both spoke at once, Harris's deeper voice overlapping hers in a way that felt oddly intimate and exposing.

Eden smiled stiffly. 'I just meant that I'm a bit of a new kid on the block.'

'But you do remind me of someone,' he said after a moment.

Obviously, he wasn't expecting her to tell the truth. Quite the opposite in fact. He was treading quietly but heavily on her toes. Which of course made her want to shout it from the rooftops because after Liam she had sworn never to be any man's dirty little secret.

In the months after their split, she had wondered why she hadn't realised the truth.

With hindsight it all seemed so glaringly obvious. For starters, he'd always been having to rush off. But she hadn't understood then that it wasn't just teenagers who had curfews. Married men had them too.

Then there were the other glaringly red flags like the fact that he'd never invited her back to his place. He'd always had an excuse. The boiler was broken. The neighbours were having work done and the builders were just so loud. And despite dating him for a year she had never met any of his friends or family.

She felt it beneath her ribs. Not anger, but a cool slippery shame, squatting there like a toad. Liam had always had excuses for that too. And for why all his calls went to voicemail.

The truth had been there in huge letters that would have been visible from space to anyone else on the planet. But she had been young, straight out of college and desperate to prove that she was immune to the same curse as all the other women in her family. That she would be able to attract that most mythical of men: the one that didn't want to get away.

Which was why nobody from her family had known about their 'relationship' either. She hadn't wanted to

jinx it by telling her mom and grandmother. She had
wanted to hold it close, to keep it precious and unsullied
because she'd been so convinced that she was different
from them, so determined that she would be the exception and not the rule.

'I have that kind of face,' she said coolly. 'People are
always thinking I look like somebody they know. It can
be a bit confusing sometimes.'

Those mesmerising grey irises were steady on her
face. 'That must be it, then.'

But it was she who'd got confused. Back in the bar,
she had sensed something raw about this man, something
intensely male, primitive almost. And it was still there,
that same compelling sensual masculinity. Only now it
was sheathed, not just in a suit that flattered every hard
contour of muscle but with the indisputable authority
of someone who was used to getting what he wanted.
And no doubt casting it aside when it no longer served
a purpose.

Her eyes darted around the quiet luxury of the lounge.
This was his natural habitat. This exclusive private mem-
bers' club with its deferential staff and expensive fur-
nishings. Because he wasn't anything like the other men
who'd been in the bar.

They were all interchangeable. Easy to read.

Easy to forget.

She felt a cool, silvery shiver like liquid mercury tremble down her spine as his eyes met hers.

Even without a name Harris Carver was not someone
you could ever forget.

'Take a seat.'

The command in his voice whipped at her senses and

she sat down in one of the leather club chairs, wishing she had worn trousers instead of a skirt as his eyes grazed her legs. She had dithered over what to wear but ended up going for a navy pinstripe pencil skirt because coupled with the heels it made her look like one of the grown-ups.

Sometimes she was so jaded with life and people and all the stupid, mean stuff they did that she felt as old as the Sphinx. But she knew that, to clients, she looked young, and they equated youth with inexperience.

It didn't help that like all the women in her family she was petite. Unfortunately, and unjustly, taller people were perceived as more authoritative, which was why she'd picked her highest heels for today's meeting.

Also, she liked the silhouette of the skirt. All that time in the gym had given her quads and glutes. Yes, it was a cliché, but at the time, when she had been reeling and wounded from Liam's betrayal, a revenge body had felt like a kind of win.

It still did. Walking into the club today, she had flexed her muscles on purpose because it reminded her that she was a survivor. That power was always there for the taking and that she was a powerful woman who had walked through fire and survived.

Looking up, she shivered inside as her eyes clashed again with his molten silver gaze. But some fires burned brighter and hotter than others.

She watched, her nerves twitching as he opened his laptop and scrolled slowly down the screen, taking his time, flexing his will as she had flexed her muscles. 'You come highly recommended, Ms Fennell.' Now he lounged back in the chair, his eyes roaming over her face, then stopping abruptly to pin her gaze just as he had in the bar.

And in the bedroom.

And in the mirror as he'd held her shoulder and watched her shudder to a climax as he'd thrust powerfully inside her.

Her skin felt hot and tingly, and she glanced away. Did he remember it too? Was she imprinted on his brain in the same way? Had he spent the last two weeks chasing shadows across the city trying to assuage that sharp, relentless ache that wouldn't soften and fade by itself?

It was impossible to tell just by looking. His face was as impenetrable as a brick wall.

'Thank you.'

He smiled but it was a smile that remained on his lips. His eyes stayed cool and hard. 'It wasn't a compliment, Ms Fennell. Just an observation.'

Her chin jerked up. Right, so that was how this was going to go.

She glanced over to where he was seated, his long legs stretched out casually. But she knew he was still furious because her turning up here had taken away his control. Here with his staff, he was the big boss. A rich, powerful, smooth-shaven, hard-talking CEO lounging like an emperor in his handmade suit and shoes. Why would he ever want them to know that there was another hungry-eyed version of him who had anonymous sex with strangers?

Was that what he usually did?

It hurt more than it should, thinking that she was just one in a long line of nameless women he'd hooked up with. It hadn't felt like that at the time. They might not have known each other's names, but there had been something there, an ease and a friction that was both contradictory and yet true. She shivered inside. That was dangerous thinking. But he had been so tempting, and she had been so tempted.

Which was why she'd left without waking him. She hadn't been sure she could resist him, and she couldn't be that needy even for a moment. Not any more.

Only it was hard, because just like every other woman in her family she craved security and certainty above all else. It was that craving that had driven her into Liam's arms, and, like moths to a flickering flame, they got burned every single time.

Her brain hiccupped as a new thought suddenly occurred to her, one that might explain why Harris was radiating such intense displeasure at her presence. Because she had left him sleeping in that hotel room, which she was pretty sure didn't happen to him very often, possibly never.

Tough! She wasn't here to manage his male pride.

Sitting up straighter, she leaned forward slightly. 'For me it's a compliment to be recommended by any of my clients,' she countered. 'Why wouldn't it be? They're all demanding, successful people with high standards.'

She felt the atmosphere in the room quiver to attention as his fingers tightened on the arm of his chair and she remembered again how they'd gripped her hip. That moment of need and recognition—

'Your client list is impressive,' he admitted begrudgingly as if he regretted admitting it. He glanced down at the screen. 'Given your age.'

She blinked.

Wow, that was condescending, and it was so tempting

to tell him that. But she was too ambitious to get mouthy with clients, even one as vexing as Harris Carver. She couldn't afford to be labelled as stroppy or difficult or thin-skinned, because all it would take was one or two stray remarks and suddenly she would have a reputation and there would be no new clients coming in.

That was the thing about human beings. They all had opinions about one another, but if enough people thought the same thing, then those opinions became your reputation.

Take her family. With her short shorts and flirty smile and paint-splattered tank tops, her mum was nothing like her friends' mothers, and her grandmother was definitely not some apple-cheeked little old lady sitting in a rocker on the porch.

But just because they ran life-drawing classes and drank beer and laughed and dated unsuitable men didn't mean they deserved to be called names.

Even as a child, when she hadn't fully understood the meaning of those names, she had wanted to make it stop. Maybe that was why she'd ended up in this job and why it felt less like a job and more a way of life.

She caught a glimpse of silver and steel and, looking up, she found Harris Carver watching her. Holding his gaze, she nodded. 'Almost as impressive as the fact that most of my clients have come to me through word-of-mouth recommendations, including those in Europe.'

Her pulse dipped as his eyes dropped to hers.

'I saw that you started out in London. An odd decision to quit the States so early in your career. Was the pond too big for you to get noticed here? Or were the other fish just that much bigger than you that you couldn't compete for food?'

Screw you, she thought, resentment surging through her.

'First off, I didn't quit, Mr Carver, and secondly, even in a capitalist economy, bigger doesn't always mean better. Sometimes "bigger" can be a disadvantage. It can encourage complacency, which in turn can lead to a stifling of imagination. That's not a criticism,' she added coolly, holding his gaze. 'It's just an observation.'

Okay, that was pretty mouthy, but he was pushing her hard, too hard.

His head of Comms smiled minutely and nodded.

Harris Carver didn't smile or nod. He just stared at her and for so long it felt as though they were in some kind of staring competition.

'You didn't answer my question.'

She lifted her chin. 'I moved to London before I started the business. My father is English, so I have dual nationality. I wanted a change and also a chance to connect with that side of my heritage.'

It was more than that. Still raw from Liam's rejection and from losing their baby, she had needed to put an ocean between herself and her memories. Moving to England had been a chance to put some literal distance between herself and her past mistakes and the pain that kept catching her unawares whenever she saw a couple with a baby. When she was surrounded by strangers her pain and shame were invisible, and that was what she'd wanted.

'Hence the accent.'

He had noticed. Not many people did. It wasn't that

pronounced but that was the difference between him and those other guys in that bar. He didn't just hear, he listened. Bluff and bluster, charm, good looks and luck, they all got you so far. But sustaining success, preserving power, only happened if you paid attention.

Which he did, she thought, her insides tightening as she remembered the soft meditative trace of his fingers. He had known instinctively where to touch her to make her squirm because he had been listening to her body, to the stagger of her breath and the noises she'd tried and failed to hold back. But he must also have taken his eye off the ball at some point otherwise she wouldn't be sitting here.

In short, he was that most compelling of all men. A contradiction, an enigma, a puzzle, and she loved solving puzzles.

Jigsaws. Crosswords. Sudoku. Whodunnits.

But complicated men had complicated lives. Sometimes they even had a whole other life with a wife in it.

Which was why she met men in bars. Why she didn't learn their names. Why she left before they could leave her. And why she was going to keep ignoring the strange, shimmering thread between her and Harris that pulled taut every time she met his glittering grey gaze.

'I do have an accent, particularly when I've been over in London for a while. There are certain words I mix up. Some spellings too. I forget where I am sometimes.'

Avery Williams smiled.

Harris Carver didn't. He didn't so much as move a muscle. Because she was watching so closely, she could see the rise and fall of his chest, but she felt something in his gaze narrow on her.

'Does that happen often? You forgetting where you are?'

The hairs on the nape of her neck shivered to attention.

She thought back to her confusion when she'd woken up in the hotel room. But that hadn't been forgetting. It was him. He had made all of it slide out of her head. Her past. Her fears. Her failures. His touch had opened her up and everything had spilled out until nothing remained except her hunger and a need for him to keep touching her.

Her heart thudded as his eyes met hers. 'Not often, no.'

She tried to pretend that the silence that followed her reply didn't get to her, but it was hard when he was watching her so closely. 'To recap, then,' he said finally. 'Your agency is small, smaller than your rivals, and you have less experience and outreach than they have. So, what exactly is it that you are bringing to the table, Ms Fennell? Other than an occasional episode of amnesia and some poor spelling.'

That grated. As it was meant to. He was needling her, trying to get a rise. To get her to trip up on her anger.

Because he wanted her gone, wanted her to walk away from this job.

But she wasn't going anywhere. This was her life. She wasn't just piggybacking on someone else's, and she wasn't going to give it up for anyone.

'I know you considered other candidates,' she said crisply. 'I'm guessing you were looking at the heavy-weights.' Her mind flashed to the boxing match. His did too. She could see it in his eyes.

'And I can't compete with them.'

'Then why are you here?' he said in that clipped, economical way of his, reminding her again, as if she needed reminding, that he was a man who was used to his opinions being treated not simply as commentary but as protocol.

'If you don't have what it takes to compete with your rivals, Ms Fennell, then I would suggest you leave now because I need someone exceptional to fight my corner.'

There was a short, sticky silence as his head of Comms stared into the middle distance. Eden felt her face grow warm.

She held her breath. Counted to ten. Then ten more.

'You misunderstand me, Mr Carver. What I was trying to explain is that I can't compete with those other agencies. Then again, I'm not trying to. I'm not criticising them. They are strategic and well connected and expert.'

She inclined her head towards Avery Williams. 'But I think it's worth pointing out that your people considered and discounted them. As they should have done, in my opinion. You see, those agencies have a reputation too. And that can be an advantage. Sometimes in situations like these just hiring the right firm can shut down the rumour mill—'

'But not in this case?' He eyed her across the room, his slate-coloured gaze as demanding as his question.

She paused. 'No. Not unless you're looking for a hard-charge, high-profile litigation—'

'I'm not.'

'Again, because you understand that it can backfire. Fan the flames of something you want extinguished.'

His gaze had sharpened, that fascinating mouth of his pursing in a facsimile of a kiss. The memory of that kiss in the rain immediately slid into her head, unprompted and intrusive, and it took a moment of concentrated effort to recover her train of thought.

'And because, like I said before, bigger is not always better. In this instance, it could actually be damaging. You're a very wealthy, powerful man but those big-name agencies have better brand recognition and that will make you look small and subservient. Never a good look, particularly when it comes to defending one's reputation,' she added, giving in once again to that childish urge to goad him as he had been goading her.

His nostrils flared, eyes locking with hers, narrowing above his uptilted chin.

'So, you're saying you'll be subservient to me.'

There was a rough edge to his voice that made her body loosen and heat bloomed low in her pelvis as she replayed the moment when he had caught her wrists and held her captive.

'I'm saying that I won't be the story here. And by the time I've finished, you won't be a story either. You talked earlier about having someone in your corner. I will be that someone. I will always be that someone because, unlike those other agencies, I only work with one client at a time. My attention will be entirely on you, twenty-four hours a day.'

She tilted her chin, mirroring his stance.

'As for all this talk of fighting—it's just a distraction. It's noise. My success will be measured by the absence of events, the absence of headlines and chatter. So, in answer to your question, what I'm offering is the quiet elevation of your reputation.'

For a moment he didn't react but then he nodded

LOUISE FULLER   61

slowly and her heart lurched. To cover her reaction, she
reached for her laptop.

'Out of interest, is the timing of this story in any way
significant?'

'Significant in what way?' he asked, grey eyes boring into her face.

'Someone has targeted you. I just wonder why and
why now. What are they getting out of it?'

He shrugged. 'I don't know. Does there need to be a
reason? I'm in the public eye. Isn't this just what hap-
pens sometimes?'

'Yes, it is. Only it doesn't happen in a vacuum, and,
more importantly, it has never happened to you before.'
Holding his gaze, she turned her laptop. 'I've just typed in
your name and nothing controversial or contentious comes
up except this one story. Which is odd, don't you think?'

'What I think is that it's one of those distractions you
say I don't need in my life.'

'So, you have no opinion as to who might have started
these rumours? Because, for example, if it's a disgruntled
employee we can—'

He held her gaze. 'It's not a disgruntled employee.'

'A rival, then? Someone who stands to gain in business terms.'

'There is Tiger McIntyre,' Avery Williams said quietly. 'He's HCI's closest competitor.'

'What difference does it make who's behind the
story?' He was still staring at her, and she had to stiffen
her neck to stop from turning her head just to escape
his gaze.

'It tells us if this is a warning shot or just a stray bul-
let.' She cleared her throat. 'Look, I understand that it's
hard for someone in your position, Mr Carver, to lose

control of their narrative but, if I am going to help you, I need you to commit, and that means being honest with me. I'm not your priest, I don't need to hear your confession, but if there is anything that could impact on your character, anything that might come to light which is pertinent, then I need you to tell me asap because further down the line it will be a far greater challenge to make it go away.'

There was a silence that made her feel as though she'd been jettisoned into space.

'There's nothing to tell.' His pupils flared as he spoke and, too late, she realised that he'd thought she was talking about what had happened between them in the hotel.

Her heart squeezed as he got to his feet abruptly.

'Thank you for coming in, Ms Fennell.' He held out his hand again and she took it reluctantly, but this time his fingers barely grazed hers before he was pulling away. He waited, impatience pulsing from every pore as she shook hands with Avery Williams, then— 'Sean, take Ms Fennell next door and arrange her security clearance.'

She watched him turn away, feeling oddly flattened.

But his PA was already on his feet, and, collecting her things, she turned and followed him out of the room. It felt like a minor triumph that she managed to do so without glancing back once. Although, really, she had more to celebrate than that. She had survived what was probably the trickiest meeting of her career. The contract was signed. All the i's had been dotted and the t's crossed.

Why, then, did everything still feel so unfinished between her and her new boss?

CHAPTER FOUR

HARRIS FELT RATHER than saw Eden Fennell leave.

He wanted to pinch himself to make absolutely sure that he wasn't in the middle of some elaborate dream but he'd already acted out of character this evening. And it was because of her. From the moment Eden had walked in, he'd felt as if everything solid and real were turning to sand.

Of course, if he'd bothered to read the report that his staff had compiled, none of this would be happening. He would have seen her photo, and he would have made an excuse to his team. Or perhaps he wouldn't. He was the boss and that was one of the perks. Never having to explain or apologise.

Either way, he would have vetoed her appointment.

Or would he?

His mind returned to the moment she had sashayed into the room in that skirt and those heels. The last time he'd seen her she was naked on the bed, her arms stretched above her head, that tempting curve of a body arching up as she offered her breasts to the heat of his mouth, so understandably it had been a shock to see her again. And even now it was almost impossible to believe that the petite, cool-eyed brunette in the pinstripe skirt and sky-high heels was the same woman who had come apart beneath him two weeks ago.

She had been shocked to see him too.

Not openly. She hadn't gasped or pressed her hand against that mouth of hers, but her eyes had widened fractionally as she'd recognised him.

He knew exactly how she'd felt, finally putting a name to a face.

To a body.

To a pulse.

He knew because he was feeling it too. That pinprick of shock like an inoculating jab and then the slow, numbing spread of disbelief.

Beside him, Avery was putting her laptop into her bag, and he could sense her confusion. He couldn't blame her. Today was supposed to have been a friendly meet and greet, and normally in these meetings, he was happy to let his team ask the questions. He preferred to watch…

His body tensed, groin hardening as he remembered watching Eden in the mirror and he had to blank his mind quickly to the image of her body shuddering against his.

'I'm sure you must be wondering why I took the lead.' He waved away Avery's protests. 'I just wanted to know she can do the job.'

Which was true, but what was truer was that the shock of Eden being there had left him feeling tricked and exposed, and he'd needed to own the room.

Own the room or own her?

Gritting his teeth, he glanced at his watch. 'I have to go. I have a dinner this evening. I'll see you tomorrow.'

'But you liked her. Ms Fennell. You think she's a good fit?'

He nodded. 'Yes, I do. You chose well.'

As he strode through the club towards the doors, he saw that his car was already idling outside, sleek and dark, the tinted windows only partially concealing his driver. Beside it, his bodyguard stood, solid and imposing.

But he wasn't looking at them, instead his gaze was fixed on the limo behind his. The one that would take Eden Fennell back to wherever she wanted to go.

Eden. He rolled the name on his tongue. Another woman, most women in fact, would find it impossible to carry off. But it suited her and not just because she was beautiful. In those few febrile hours they'd shared together there had been a wildness to her and a lack of inhibition that had transformed that simple hotel room into a paradise of pleasure.

Today though she was poised and aloof, and that aloofness had wound him up. That was why he'd been so hard on her. He had wanted to see that flare of passion again, so he'd pushed her on every point. But she'd held her ground. Pushed back, he thought, remembering the snippy remark she'd made about him being small and subservient.

He gritted his teeth. This was the second time Eden Fennell had knocked him off balance and left him scrambling to make sense of his world.

But things had changed.

She was working for him now and the sooner she realised what that meant, the better it would be for both of them. Waving away his bodyguard, he stalked over to the second limo. She wasn't in it, so she was probably still sorting out her security clearance.

By the time Eden appeared through the doors, he was back in control, lounging against his car, his eyes ostensibly on his phone but he knew exactly when she caught sight of him because he saw her falter.

'Ms Fennell—'

'Mr Carver—'

She was walking towards him now, her eyes steady on his face and he felt another tiny jolt of admiration and a curiosity that rarely troubled him when it came to women. But there was usually nothing to be curious about. Women liked him because he was rich and good-looking, and he liked them because they were beautiful, willing and endlessly available.

His jaw clenched and he had a sudden vivid memory of waking alone in that bed, and of reaching across the mattress to find nothing. He couldn't think of one woman who would even have contemplated walking away from him.

Except this one. Who wasn't even looking at him, he realised with a flicker of irritation. Instead, she was turning slightly, frowning at the tail lights of the departing limo.

'Was that—'

'Your car? Yes.' He nodded. 'I told the driver to leave. No point taking two cars when mine is heading in the same direction.'

She didn't like that. Even before she spun round towards him, he could feel the annoyance snap down her spine.

'I doubt that. I don't live in the Upper East Side.'

'Then it's lucky for you that I'm not going to the Upper East Side.' He held her gaze. 'Look, it'll be a small diversion for my driver, and it's good for the environment too. Besides, we need to talk,' he added.

'You just spent an hour grilling me. I think that's enough talking, don't you?' She reached into her bag and pulled out a phone. 'You go ahead. I'll call a cab.'

'Just get in the car, Ms Fennell. It's a ten-minute drive. I mean, what are you scared of?'

'Not much. Spiders. Snakes. The occasional very big beetle.' Angling her chin, she looked up at him in that cool, taunting way of hers. 'You know, if fear is how you motivate your staff, Mr Carver, I'm surprised that this is your first reputational crisis.'

'And I'm surprised you need any motivation to have a brief conversation with your boss. What was it you said about being in my corner? Something about my having your attention twenty-four hours a day? Yet here you are quibbling over giving me ten minutes of your time.'

Her green eyes flashed, and she glanced away because he was right, and she hated that. He loved that he could read her reaction so easily now, because she had spent the last hour keeping her emotions in check—keeping him in check.

'Perhaps I didn't make myself clear. I'm very happy to have a conversation of any length with you. But only if it doesn't involve you making accusations about why we ended up in bed.'

He swore under his breath. 'And *that* is exactly why we need to talk.'

She held his gaze as he took a step forward and he felt another reluctant flicker of admiration. He was six foot three. She barely reached his shoulders yet here she was staring him down.

'Fine,' she said coolly. 'You can take me to Cooper Square. I have a hotel room just off there.'

She did?

Then why had they rented another one that night?

But she was already sidestepping past him, opening the door on the passenger side, slamming it after herself before that thought had finished formulating, and he laughed. It was either that or pull her back out of the car and kiss her until she accepted that they were doing things his way—

'Mr Carver?'

His driver's voice snapped him back into his body and, feeling exposed and annoyed that Eden could make him feel that way, he turned and said curtly, 'Change of plan, Owen. We're taking Ms Fennell back to her hotel first.'

Yanking open the other door, he slid onto the seat beside Eden and, having stretched out his legs, he turned to where she was sitting stiffly.

She spoke first. 'So that's what this is about? You think I'm going to go and tell everyone what happened?'

Their gazes collided. No, she wouldn't do that, he thought, without missing a beat. Inside the club just now, she had been eloquent—but that was business.

How many words had she spoken to him before they'd left the bar? Thirty maybe. Less than that in the hotel. But by then, they'd had other things on their minds aside from conversation.

He shrugged. 'It crossed my mind,' he lied.

She glanced away. 'Well, uncross it. I'm not a fan of blabbing about my private life to anyone and I don't expect you to do it either.' Her head turned slightly, enough for her green eyes to pierce him, steady, determined, proud. 'What happened that night was between us.'

Us. The word vibrated inside him. He had never managed to be a 'we' or an 'us' with any woman. How could you be something that you fundamentally didn't understand?

Sex was different. There was nothing to understand. It was hormones, pheromones, biology. You didn't need to learn it; it was a primal urge, an instinct. And some relationships were instinctive too, or they were supposed to be. Parents were programmed to love their children, to want to protect and nurture and indulge them.

Not in his family.

His chest tightened with the old, familiar mix of fury and bafflement and pain. Logically, he could see why it had been like that. His parents had nothing in common with each other except one night of cheap beer and careless sex. They hadn't wanted to marry. They certainly hadn't wanted a baby. But that was what they'd got. And maybe in the beginning, they had thought that against all odds they could make it work. Or maybe they had simply been marking time until they could get divorced. Either way, despite being man and wife they'd not been a couple except in name only.

Yet, the strange thing was that even though he and Eden had spent only six hours together at most, they had felt like an 'us'. And he'd felt at one with himself, and with her, in a way that was absent from any other relationship he could remember.

Which was probably why his daughter was being raised by another man on the other side of the world.

'Is that why you wanted to talk to me? Because I meant what I said. My private life is private.'

He nodded. 'But you can understand why I would have concerns. I don't need any more bad publicity.'

There was a lengthy pause.

'As your reputation manager, I can only concur.' Another pause. 'I just didn't know that's what I was.'

He shook his head. 'You misunderstand me—'

She shrugged. 'What's to understand? You like to pick up women in bars for sex.'

Her directness surprised him enough to tell the truth. 'I usually don't, and you picked me up.'

He felt his body respond to the sudden heat in her eyes. 'Whatever.' She shrugged. 'It doesn't matter either way.'

'Is that why you left before I woke up?' He spoke unthinkingly, her absence still a raw wound, but as her chin jerked up, he felt a tiny stab of satisfaction that he had got beneath her skin even if it came at the cost of her having got beneath his.

'I had something to do.' Her voice was fierce, and he felt a sudden compulsion to ask her what could have been more important than their feverish need for each other.

'And you paid for the room—'

'Why does that matter?'

Good question, he thought, only it was one that he couldn't easily answer even though he was feeling the same sense of shock and outrage as before, the same irritation with himself for minding so much about something so trivial. But any answer he gave would make him look like some Neanderthal throwback. She would think it was his ego.

And it was, but not because he needed to pick up the bill to feel like a man.

It cut deeper than that. He had felt that same sense of being surplus to requirements. Maybe if they'd had a conversation about it, he would have let her pay if that was what she wanted, although that in itself was mind-boggling. He couldn't remember the last time a woman had offered to pay for anything.

But she hadn't talked to him. She had simply paid and left.

Just like Jessie. Only she had bought an air ticket back home to Australia.

Aged eighteen, he had been relieved. Relieved? It shouldn't hurt that much when something was true, but he felt a hot wave of shame and anger rise up inside him and although his voice was quiet when he finally answered her, it cost him.

'I'd already given them my credit card details.'

'I know, but I wanted to pay.' She frowned. 'I don't see what your problem is. Surely, you're not so old-fashioned that you can't let a woman pay for a hotel room.'

'I'm not old-fashioned—'

'Then what's the big deal? Yes, I paid, but before that you left your credit-card details so how is that any different?'

'Because you were there. You saw me do it. You had a chance then to say how you wanted things to be.'

Unlike him. He had been sidelined his entire life, first by his parents and then by the mother of his child. Not that Eden Fennell needed to know about any of that.

'I'd have preferred to be consulted.'

Yet another pause.

'Would you have hired me if you had been?'

He felt a pang as he remembered the remark he'd made when he'd introduced her to Avery.

'I mean, if you had realised who I was?'

He glanced over to where she was sitting. In the subdued lighting of the car, she looked defiant and young. She was young, he reminded himself, remembering her date of birth from the résumé Avery had sent him. The same age he'd been when he'd finally had the money to start trying to track down Jasmine. By then, he'd felt so old, as if he'd lived a hundred lives.

'Probably not,' he admitted. 'But I trust Avery. She has good instincts and you presented well today.'

'I know it must feel like you're taking a risk but I'm very good at my job.'

'I hope you're better than good. In fact, I expect the best and by that I mean I want this process to feel organic, not staged in any way.'

'Of course.' She nodded. 'Don't worry. I won't have you judging best in show at the county fair or kissing babies—'

It was instantly and shockingly, piercingly painful, just as if she'd leaned over and punched him in the face. Because it didn't matter how many years had passed. In fact, with every year that passed, it was getting harder and harder to not think about his daughter because she was always in his heart.

Beside him, Eden shifted forward. 'I will do a good job for you. I'm not a quitter.' There was a different note to her voice now, a certainty and a confidence that made her seem older than twenty-five.

'I'll hold you to that.'

Outside the car, the city was changing tempo. The rhythm of the night was starting to overlap the end of the working day.

He felt the memory of that night lap up against his skin and, even though she was sitting on the other side of the limo, he felt crowded by his need for her. His fingers twitched as she looked over at him, her pupils huge and dark, holding him steady, and he felt the combative tension between them dissolving like salt in warm water.

Glancing away, she cleared her throat. 'This is fine for me.'

He tapped on the privacy screen and the limo pulled smoothly alongside the kerb.

'I'll send a car to pick you up in the morning. Be ready for eight.'

'No need. I know where your office is, Mr Carver.'

He shook his head. 'The paparazzi are already sniffing around the building.'

'I can take care of myself.'

His chest tightened sharply as he pictured her trying to push her way through a baying pack of photographers and journalists. 'Take the car, Eden, and that's an order.' It was the first time he had spoken her name out loud, and he felt something loosen in him as her chin jerked up and their gazes locked momentarily, her green eyes clear and startled. Then she was opening the door and stepping onto the pavement.

She didn't look back and after a few seconds she was swallowed up by the crowds. As the car began to move, he found his gaze pulling towards the window. But that was understandable, he told himself. He was still coming to terms with her sudden reappearance. It was frustrating that just when he needed to be most stable, he was feeling so unfettered, so like a stranger to himself.

Tomorrow would be different.

By then he would no longer be in shock, and if they spent more time together then Eden would become a woman like any other and stop feeling like some fantasy who had sprung unexpectedly and distractingly to life.

Leaning back against the headrest, he deliberately closed his eyes. Everything was under control, and he fully expected that in a matter of weeks his reputation would be, if not fully restored, then well on the way to it. Finally, he would be able to put this whole disastrous episode behind him.

And that night in the hotel would be nothing more than a half-remembered dream.

His expectations had proved correct, he thought a week later as he stepped out of the elevator on the executive level. Except on one account. His mouth formed around a four-letter word.

Eden.

It had been a promising theory, thinking that proximity and familiarity could dull the senses, and with every other woman of his acquaintance it had swiftly and effortlessly become reality. But not with her.

It was almost the end of the working day and most of his staff were picking up their coats and bags. A few were chatting. Others were heading towards the elevator.

Soon the office would be empty and quiet. He liked it like that. Liked watching the sun set from his office. Some days, most days if he was being truthful, it felt more•like home than his glittering, echoing triplex. Particularly at the moment. He seemed drawn here, coming in earlier, staying later than usual, returning when there was really no reason to do so.

The lie fizzed inside his head. There was a reason. He was looking at her now.

His stride faltered infinitesimally as his gaze narrowed in on Eden, and that was annoying in itself. There were any number of brunettes currently working at HCI and yet without exception every time he walked into the open-plan office, his eyes seemed to find their way to her unerringly like a heat-seeking missile.

Although he couldn't put his finger on why.

It wasn't as if she dressed outlandishly.

Take today. She was wearing another of those silky blouses and a pair of slim-fitting trousers, and that his brain had even registered that blew his mind. He wasn't remotely interested in women's clothing and usually had no opinion on what they wore. But he could pretty much remember every single outfit Eden had worn this week and all of them seemed to have been designed with the express purpose of hinting at what they appeared to hide.

He watched her leaning forward to look at something on Avery's laptop, her hair falling to cover her profile, and he felt a flash of regret that he could no longer see the curve of her jaw.

The two women were talking intently and then Avery's assistant, Aaron, came over and said something and Eden nodded and smiled, and he felt his insides clench. She had a sweet smile, natural and warming like spring sunshine. Not that he'd experienced it first-hand. The smiles she reserved for him were polite and perfectly calibrated to reveal nothing and he suddenly found himself willing her to look over and smile at him like that.

Harris Carver was back.

Eden didn't look up, but she didn't need to see him to know he was there. Her body had already quivered to attention like a dog hearing its owner's car in the drive and as she felt him walk towards her, the noises in the office seemed to fade away and she was aware of nothing beyond the pounding of her heart.

And his eyes.

When finally she could no longer bear it, she looked up. Her throat tightened. He was staring down at her, those grey eyes of his boring into her like the drills he was designing for the moon.

'Mr Carver—'

'Ms Fennell.'

He inclined his head slightly and she gave him one of her specially patented you're-the-boss smiles that she had been pinning to her face for the last five days.

'You seem very focused on something. What are you thinking about?'

You, she thought, her eyes zigzagging down over his body. Every mesmerising inch of him. Ever since he'd dropped her off in Cooper Square, she had spent too many hours to bill researching him, and usually that was the part she enjoyed the most. Not just because it gave her the foundation stones to build a strategy. There was something relaxing about research. It was like doing a jigsaw puzzle.

Except in Harris's case, it felt as though there were

multiple missing pieces and others that simply didn't fit into any of the holes.

His media footprint up until the *Chronicle* story was incredibly light. There were no puff pieces, hardly any interviews and the biography his Comms teams had given her could be best described as minimalist.

She had other ways of researching her clients. Eavesdropping on staff as they congregated around the water cooler or waited for the elevators or even in the restrooms. None of which had revealed much that she didn't already know.

The data from the social listening company had hinted at a rivalry between Harris and Tiger McIntyre, which tied in with what Avery had said at that first meeting, but it was mostly uncredited fragments of supposition.

Still, she found herself poring over every detail like some teenager reading fan fiction about her favourite character so that even when her laptop powered down in exhaustion, he was there inside her head. Worse, when she finally made it to bed, as she fell asleep, Harris would still be there beside her, his arm pressing her tightly against him, his heat spreading through her limbs.

So that was relaxing.

She cleared her throat. 'This is the mentoring website. It's not completely finished but I'm really pleased with it.'

'Come into my office and I'll take a look,' he said, picking up her laptop and snapping it shut as he walked off. She stared after him for a moment, then followed him reluctantly as he must have known she would, not least because she needed her laptop back.

'So, when does it go live?'

'The morning you visit the school. We're letting them

manage all the publicity so it will be quite basic and amateurish but that's what we want. And it won't stop the story getting picked up by the mainstream media outlets.'

'Isn't that a bit risky? What if it doesn't?'

'It will. Your name guarantees that, but we want it to look authentic. It has to feel organic and speak to your character. Otherwise, I might as well have you jumping out of a cake in swim shorts waving fistfuls of dollars and pledging your support for orphans and widows.'

'You don't see me doing that?' His gaze had risen to meet hers, sharper than before, as if he wanted to watch her reply, and then his mouth pulled minutely at the corners, and she had to press her feet into the polished concrete floor to stop from turning and running out of his office. Because that ghost of a smile made her feel blurred at the edges as if she were melting...

She shook her head partly to answer his question but mostly because she hoped it would hide her reaction from his all-seeing gaze. 'Funnily enough, no.'

His eyes drifted down to where the pulse in her throat was beating in time to an invisible pair of castanets and in desperation she spun round slowly.

'This is a beautiful space.'

It wasn't the first time she had been in this office but before there had been other people and there hadn't been much time to take in her surroundings. It was predictably and impressively large. What was less predictable was the artwork.

She stared up at the pictures on the wall. She had been in other offices of wealthy, successful business leaders. There was a definite decor among the superrich. They liked clean lines and high ceilings and tall windows. And they loved art.

Old Masters. Impressionists. Picasso. Pollock. Rothko. Hirst.

But this man had drawings. Not the Michelangelo kind. Technical drawings of machinery. Blueprints for the future of humanity. She peered forward.

'It's a motor driver. For the lunar rover we designed.'

Harris's voice made her jump inside her skin. Steadying her breathing, she said over her shoulder, 'Are you included in that "we"?'

'I understand the components and the engineering, and I probably could design something fairly basic, but nothing like that. Not any more. And I don't have to. HCI have teams of designers who will do it for me. But I like to be involved.'

'And consulted,' she said softly.

He had moved closer while she was looking at the pictures and, glancing up, she felt his intent gaze and the latent power of his body envelop her.

'That too.'

She licked her lips and forced her attention back to the drawings. 'Are they special in some way? Is that why you have them in your office?'

'Some are. That one.' He pointed to the print on her left. 'That one was the first of our designs to make it up to the International Space Station. It's a safety tether, which is a basic piece of kit for astronauts. Essential, really, if they don't want to join all the other space junk orbiting the Earth. Others, I just like the look of them because there's something pleasing about the ratio of straight lines to curves.'

'Like this one.' She pointed to a different print. 'That's probably my favourite.'

'Mine too,' he said quietly. 'It's a pistol grip drill.'

She glanced at the scale at the bottom of the drawing. 'It must be quite big in real life.'

'It is. It has to be, because of the gloves the astronauts wear. But it's made of glass-coated plastic covered in aluminium so it's light.'

'Do you ever get to see the finished product?'

He nodded. 'I do. I see all the various prototypes before they go into production. And we get sent footage of them in situ.'

She frowned. 'You mean on the moon?'

He shook his head. 'Not currently, but in the future. Right now, we have around thirty products in operational use on the space station.'

There was an odd note to his voice, guarded almost, and she was suddenly desperate to ask him why, but then she came to her senses and moved over to the window, her gaze tilting automatically up to the darkening sky. 'Is it visible from here? The space station, I mean. Or do you need a telescope?'

He shook his head. 'No telescope required. It's a bright white pinpoint of light. Typically, it's the brightest object in the sky aside from the moon. In fact, we might even be able to see it now.'

'How do you know that?'

'I get alerts about its location, and I noticed that it was passing over New York tonight.' He stared up through the glass. 'It's there. No, lower.' She felt his hand touch her shoulder, his touch light but emphatic, guiding her forward, closer to the glass so that she had to tip back her head. 'Look along my arm.'

The fabric of his sleeve was smooth against her cheek, and she could feel the press of his biceps and her heart twitched as she breathed in his scent. He smelled so good—

'I can see it.' Smiling triumphantly, she turned, and he smiled too, and she was about to turn away again, but her hand had somehow ended up pressed against his chest, and his hand was in her hair, and it was suddenly an effort to stay standing. His grey gaze was about an inch away from her, pressing into her like hot steel. Except it wasn't grey because his eyes were all pupils. Soft and dark and as fathomless as a black hole.

She could feel their gravitational pull. Or maybe that was his scent. Or the heat of his body.

Either way, she could feel herself leaning in, and she knew it was dangerous because she wasn't wearing a safety tether. If she got close enough there would be no pulling back—

'Sorry, Mr Carver—'

They both jumped apart as the light flicked on, blinding white, the intimacy dissolving like a broken spell. It was one of the security guards. 'I'm sorry, sir, I didn't know anyone was in here.'

'It's fine, Ted. I was showing Ms Fennell the Space Station, but she was just leaving—'

Eden blinked up at him. She felt like Titania waking from her enchanted sleep. 'Yes, I should be going.'

'Have a good weekend,' he said, and there was a trace of impatience in his voice along with a roughness that scraped over her skin, making her feel hot and flustered and unsteady on her feet.

'You too.'

He nodded, but he was already staring back up at the night sky, and she walked quickly towards the door before she did something stupid and regrettable. Even worse than standing in the dark alone with this incomparably beautiful man whose presence kicked up dangerous sparks in her.

Sparks that should remind her that it was dangerous to play with fire. As if she needed reminding.

CHAPTER FIVE

'IF YOU WOULD follow me, Mr Carver, Ms Fennell.'

Eden turned away from the line of lockers and smiled at Principal Evans. 'Sorry, being back at high school is giving me flashbacks.'

The principal smiled. 'I'm sure you were the model pupil, Ms Fennell.'

That was true academically. She had studied hard and been a high achiever. But outside class, things were a little trickier. She hadn't been a troublemaker as such, but you couldn't have a mother like hers and not end up with a target on your back so there had been quite a few altercations with the 'mean girls' at her school.

A few with some of the boys too. Boys who saw her mother's long legs in their short shorts and thought 'like mother like daughter'. It was one of the things that had first attracted her to Liam. He hadn't been interested in her family or her background; he'd told her that it was just her and him and it had been exactly what she'd wanted to hear.

Of course, he had only said that to justify keeping his own life secret for the very obvious reason that he was married.

Her stupidity made her squirm and, pushing away the

memory, she shook her head. 'I wish. What about you, Mr Carver? How were your schooldays?'

Probably he'd been valedictorian, and quarterback for the school team, she thought, picturing his broad shoulders in a football shirt. No doubt he'd dated a cheerleader. Most likely, all of them.

Beside her, Harris's smooth stride stuttered for perhaps a tenth of a second. Not enough to draw the attention of Principal Evans or his security detail, who were keeping pace discreetly alongside them.

But she'd noticed even though she didn't want to. Her eyes were drawn to him, always, and not just her eyes. Whenever he was present, it was as if each of her five senses was tuned to the way he moved and to the shifting tones in his voice and when he left the room, everything seemed to go staticky inside her head so that she had to really concentrate on even simple tasks.

His grey eyes were cool and clear as he shrugged. 'I don't really have any strong memories either way. Once something is over, I prefer to look forward.'

She heard the warning in his words, but he really didn't need to bother. Since that moment in his office when they'd almost kissed, he had been stiffly formal and careful to keep his distance. It was stupid to feel hurt. They'd had sex once, and it wasn't as if she wanted anything from him, like a relationship or a future. Which was lucky, because today was the final day of her contract.

She should be pleased, and proud. Everything had, not just gone as she'd hoped, but exceeded her expectations. Quietly and by stealth, Harris Carver's name had disappeared from the news headlines.

Today was his chance to reclaim his narrative.

'We're set up in the gym.' The principal smiled apologetically. 'I know that the scheme is for the senior school, but there's been so much excitement about you coming in to talk, so I hope you don't mind, Mr Carver, but we decided to let the lower years join us.'

The gym was packed. As well as the pupils, the entire staff appeared to be there too, but then it wasn't often that you got up close to a real life, self made billionaire. And Harris Carver was worth the entrance fee. He not only looked the part, but also had that aura of power and confidence that shrank the huge hall so that it felt like an average-sized room.

He was a good speaker too, despite not having received any coaching. She had checked that with him beforehand, but it seemed that he instinctively understood how to connect with an audience, speaking to the back of the room, fluently and without a script.

'Do you think Mr Carver might take some questions?' Principal Evans was looking at her hopefully when Harris finished.

She had anticipated this, and prepped Harris. Private schools might frequently get speakers like Harris Carver but for a public school, particularly one in a deprived neighbourhood like the Wendell Wells Academy High School, this was the rarest of opportunities.

Glancing at her watch, she nodded. 'Fifteen minutes, and then we really will have to go.'

The questions were the typical kind of random, unfiltered ones that teens asked.

'Do you have a private jet?'

'Are you going to run for president?'

'What's the most expensive thing you've ever bought?'

Above the roof of the gymnasium, she could hear the telltale thwapping sound of a helicopter hovering. She tilted her head slightly. Several helicopters, in fact. Which meant the news of Harris's presence had leaked out as she'd known it would. She felt his gaze seek her out, so he had heard them too. After a moment, his mouth pulled up ever so slightly at the corners and she felt his approval shiver through her like a light summer breeze and she had to actively stop herself from just grinning like a fool.

'Hi, Mr Carver. My name is Alyssa and I wanted to ask you if you ever wanted to be an astronaut.'

There was a pause. 'No, I never wanted to do that,' Harris said slowly.

'But why not?' Alyssa frowned. She looked baffled and Eden could understand why. Even without the space-suit, with his carved bone structure and cropped blond hair, he looked exactly like a Hollywood version of an astronaut. 'I think going into space would be so cool.'

'It is cool, Alyssa, but astronauts have to be a very specific kind of person. I'm not sure I'm that person. In some ways, I hope I'm not.'

There was a tension in his shoulders, as if he were carrying some invisible weight, but then it had been a long three weeks. She glanced at her watch. The helicopters would have got here first but it would be the news crews on the ground next and she didn't want this to turn into a circus. Tapping the principal on the arm, she said quietly, 'Let's make that the last question.'

'That went well.'

'It did.' Harris turned and nodded. The tension in his shoulders seemed to have lifted.

'Three of the news channels have already covered the visit and it's extremely positive. I have the links. I'll send them over to you.'

'Thank you. And thank you for all your hard work.' He hesitated. 'As you know, I had my doubts about whether this was a good idea, you working for me—'

'Working *with* you,' she said firmly but without any heat.

His eyebrow lifted. 'I was concerned that you might have overpromised but you've more than delivered.'

'You were easier to work with than I thought you'd be,' she said after a moment.

'You sound surprised.'

'Not surprised, but it can be hard to speak truth to power.'

'I didn't notice you struggling.' He smiled in a way that made her feel grateful she was sitting down.

'I did tell you that we needed to be honest with each other if this relationship was going to work,' she said.

'You did. But it seems a little one-sided. I mean, I know next to nothing about you.'

He was being polite or passing the time. It meant nothing, but she felt panic ripple through her like quicksilver and she couldn't tell if it was because she wanted to keep herself hidden from him or, more confusingly, to tell him the truth.

'Not much to know. I grew up in San Antonio. Went to school, college. Graduated, went to—'

'Went to England,' he finished her sentence. 'Started the business. Do you want me to list your clients? Because I can. It's all on your résumé, which I've read.'

'The trailer is the best way to sell a film,' she said,

keeping her voice light and casual. 'I don't want to bore you with the four-hour director's cut.'

He waited, and she held her breath, hoping he'd move on.

Damn, he was good at waiting.

She sighed theatrically because it gave her a chance to adjust her breathing. 'Okay, I'll trade you. You ask me one thing that's not on my résumé and I get to ask you one thing.'

'I've already told you so much—'

'Yeah, stuff I can read on the Internet.'

'Fine.' He made a surrendering movement with his hands. 'We each get one question.'

She should have tacked on some conditions, she realised as he leaned back, his grey gaze lingering on her face as if the answer were already there even though he hadn't asked his question yet.

'So, what made you go into this business?'

Was that it? She had half expected him to ask her something more personal than that. She knew she could have lied or dissembled about the things that made her feel exposed and stupid, but Harris had a way of looking at her that pulled memories and feelings to the surface. If one had come loose, she'd been scared the rest would come tumbling out like water pushing through a breaking dam.

'I don't know. I suppose I don't like injustice.'

'Meaning?'

'That's two questions.'

Her breath caught as he leaned back into the upholstery and stretched out his long legs. And waited.

She shrugged. 'I don't like people name-calling and

lying and getting away with it. It's not fair, or right.' Her stomach knotted as she remembered how people had spoken about her sweet, hopeless mother and grandmother.

'Why not be a lawyer? A litigator?'

'That's four questions.'

His mouth curved up infinitesimally. 'Three. I was just qualifying what kind of lawyer.'

'It takes twenty years to build a reputation, and five minutes to lose it. But it takes something in between to get a case to court and I don't want to get bogged down in weeks and months of he said/she said. I want to make a difference in real time. No.' She held up her hand like a police officer stopping traffic. 'It's my turn now, okay?'

Looking over to where he sat lounging casually, her stomach fluttered with nerves and anticipation. There were so many things she wanted to ask him. Quite a few were unaskable out loud, like *what did you think of me when you saw me in that bar*? Or *do you still dream about that night*?

And then suddenly she thought back to the moment in the gym when he'd hesitated. 'Did you really never want to be an astronaut?'

For a moment he said nothing, just stared past her, but he didn't need to say anything for her to know that his mood had changed. His features looked granite hard, and the easy warmth of moments earlier had faded from his eyes.

'I'm not in the habit of lying to schoolchildren,' he said slowly.

'I wasn't accusing you of lying. I was just surprised that it wasn't a dream of yours.'

'A dream?'

His anger caught her off guard but, in the light streaming through the windows of the limo, his grey eyes were shadows that offered no explanation for his sudden flash of rage. 'Why would you think that choosing a dark, lifeless vacuum over everything on Earth would be a dream of mine?' His skin was taut across his cheekbones. 'It shouldn't be anyone's dream.'

She thought back to how they'd looked up at the night sky together, his body hard and hot against hers. It was stupid, but it felt as though he'd lied to her. 'But you get alerts from the space station—'

'I track it because a lot of our equipment is up there.'

That was probably true, but she knew instinctively that he wasn't telling her the whole truth. Only what was there to lie about?

'You just seemed to know a lot about space, and usually when people are that informed it's because they're interested. So—'

'So, you presumed to think you know me.' Abruptly he leaned forward. 'Three weeks. That's how much time we've spent together. Do you think that's long enough to know someone?'

'Three weeks and one night,' she said coolly. 'And yes, I do think that's long enough. Three weeks is pretty much all I ever have to get to know clients. I can't do my job if I don't know them because I don't have a one-size-fits-all strategy, not even in a niche industry like yours. Or do you think I would use the same strategy for you as I would for Tiger McIntyre?'

She hadn't picked that name by chance. The two men were in direct competition, and they were like chalk and cheese. There were also those rumours of a long-standing rivalry. It felt like an unsurprising choice, so she was shocked by the stunned expression on Harris's face. Actually, he looked more shaken than stunned.

'What has Tiger McIntyre got to do with any of this?'

'He's your biggest competitor.'

'He is *nothing* like me.'

'That's not what I said—'

'Then perhaps you should say what you mean.'

'Oh, I don't think you want me to do that, Mr Carver,' she said stiffly, after a taut, electric moment that left her feeling shaky and singed. 'You might not like what I say.'

His eyes narrowed. 'Then it's fortunate our time together is at an end and that our lives were only briefly, and out of necessity, connected.' Shrugging up his shirt sleeve, he glanced at his watch. 'I have a conference call at four, but we can meet afterwards for the review.'

The review meeting was short and without incident. Avery gushed over her approach and her insight. Harris Carver thanked her politely for her work and she thanked him just as politely for giving her the chance to prove herself, and then they shook hands and she left.

It wasn't as if she'd expected flowers. Most of her clients were grateful and relieved in equal measure when she started working with them but, by the end, their relief typically outweighed their gratitude because they had regained control of their lives.

'He's got a lot on today but he's very pleased with you,' Avery said as they made their way back to the office Eden had been using during her time at HCI. 'I'm just going to freshen up and then we can head down to the lounge.'

Eden blinked. 'To do what?'

'There's a party. Not for you,' she added, laughing as she caught sight of Eden's no doubt appalled expression. 'Cathy's going on maternity leave on Monday so we're just giving her a little send-off.'

'That's very kind of you to invite me, Avery, but I'm not—'

'Nonsense,' Avery said firmly. 'You've been like one of the team, and, besides, Cathy asked specifically if you would come. I know you wouldn't want to disappoint a heavily pregnant woman—'

Growing up in a house full of women, she had always felt part of a sisterhood, but after losing her baby it had been hard at first to celebrate other women's pregnancies. Sometimes she'd had to physically look away from their bumps. It was still hard, but she liked Cathy a lot and she wouldn't be happy with herself if she didn't go.

'Okay, then, you've twisted my arm.'

She was still getting used to being part of a team. At school she had been a bit of a loner. University was better in terms of feeling that people had accepted her for herself but by then she had already been so guarded. Liam's deceit and abandonment had left her warier, and wearier, than ever. But she had enjoyed working here.

The party was in full flow by the time they arrived.

'Wow, there's waitstaff.'

'HCI isn't a family business, but we try and take care of our staff,' Avery said proudly. 'Mr Carver has always been very clear about that. And generous too.'

'Would you like some champagne?' One of the waiters was leaning in with a tray of glasses. 'Or we have a non-alcoholic elderflower fizz?'

'Actually, what I'd really like is a cup of tea. Milk, no sugar.' She smiled sheepishly at Avery. 'I know, but I always miss it when I first come back to the States.'

Avery smiled. 'If that's how you want to celebrate. And you should be celebrating, Eden. You did an amazing job.'

She smiled at Avery. She liked the head of Comms. Avery was a role model from an older generation, but she had championed a younger woman, which was inspiring.

'I would say I'd love to work for you again, but I think that's the last thing either of us would want.'

Avery shook her head, serious suddenly. 'You're a good fit for HCI. If I had a staff job, I'd be offering it to you now.'

'Thank you, I'd love to work for you. You have a great team.'

'Well, Harris is a great boss.'

Eden felt her smile stiffen. Avery was not alone. Everyone at HCI thought the same. But then look at Liam. Presumably his wife and friends all thought he was one of the good guys too. Or maybe they didn't, and she was the only mug to think he was perfect. Either was a depressing thought. Maybe that was why she felt so deflated, and the party felt less like a celebration and more like a marking of the end of things.

But then, after three weeks of working long into the evenings, it was the end. No wonder she felt so shattered.

Her eyes flicked to the door as she caught a glimpse of broad shoulders, her stomach flipping, but it wasn't Harris. She knew he wasn't going to appear. That weird conversation in his office with Avery standing there like a chaperone was going to be the outro to this strange, shimmering episode in her life. And it was for the best, she told herself firmly. But just the same her gaze jerked over to the door as it opened again.

Not him.

'Shall we grab something to eat?' Avery was looking at her curiously and, pulling her gaze away from the door, Eden shook her head. 'I think I might skip the food. I'm catching a flight in a couple of hours.'

'To London?'

'San Antonio. To see my family. It's a surprise.'

That was another consequence of Liam getting back in touch like that. It had reminded her of the secrecy surrounding their relationship, the lies she'd told her family, and she had felt all that remembered guilt on top of her new guilt for not confiding in them. She wanted to make amends now that the shock and pain of his revelation were no longer visible on her face.

She took a sip of her tea and frowned. It tasted weird.

The milk at home had been off too. Maybe it was the weather. She'd read somewhere that thunderstorms could curdle milk and there had certainly been plenty of those over the last few weeks.

Like the one the night she and Harris had run to the hotel.

Pushing aside the memory, she walked over to Cathy.

'You look incredible,' she said as they hugged. Cathy looked just like one of those women who modelled for pregnancy stores online. Her hair was lustrous, and her skin had a kind of luminous quality to it as if it were being lit from the inside.

Cathy smiled. 'You should have seen me seven months ago. I had all these breakouts, and my hair was greasy. I was so tired all the time and everything tasted weird. I kept throwing away stuff because I thought it had gone off.'

The door opened again, but this time, Eden didn't turn to look. Instead, she stared at Cathy, a cool, clammy panic trickling down her spine.

'Would you excuse me a moment?' She smiled. 'I'm just going to nip to the cloakroom.'

She managed to keep the smile in place right up until she shut the cubicle door. Pulling out her phone, she checked her period tracker. Everything had been so crazy since she'd arrived in New York and she'd lost track of time.

Even using her longest cycle, she was still two weeks late.

Two weeks.

Don't panic, she told herself quickly, pushing back against the memory of Harris. His hand gripping her shoulder. Breath hard and hot against her throat. A dark flush along his cheekbones and that storm of passion in his eyes.

But they had used a condom.

Trying to steady her breathing, she leaned against the wall, wishing the cool bricks could soothe her fevered brain enough to think straight. Ever since she'd opened the office in New York her cycle had been all over the place. Her friend, Lauren, who was a doctor, had told her that flying long haul could sometimes do that.

She ran her tongue over her teeth, trying to shift that metallic taste. Trying not to remember the last time she'd tasted it, trying to stem the panicky thoughts swelling up and filling her chest.

So do a test. There was no harm in checking. In fact, it would put her mind at rest, she thought as she returned to the party, and picked up her bag.

'You're not leaving, are you?' It was Cathy.

'Sorry, yes.' She held out her phone. 'It's a bit of a family emergency,' she lied. 'But I've got your socials, so I'll keep an eye open for any announcements—'

She glanced across the room and froze. Harris Carver was talking to Avery, but he was watching her. Her heart began to beat like a jackhammer. Earlier when she was talking to Avery, she had been scanning the room for him because she was stupid enough to want to see him again just one last time, but now the idea of talking to him, being in his orbit, made her feel hot and dizzy, and cornered.

'Are you okay?' Cathy was staring at her anxiously. 'You look really pale. Do you want to sit down?'

'I'm fine,' she lied. 'It's just been a long day. I have to go, but take care—'

She broke off. Harris Carver was moving purposefully across the room, and, snatching up her bag, she turned and made her way to the door.

'Eden—'

She darted out of the room and narrowly caught the elevator. But as the doors closed, she caught a glimpse of his narrowed grey, questioning gaze.

She stopped off at a drugstore on her way back to her apartment. Twenty minutes and one test later she was standing in the bathroom in just her blouse and bra, staring dazedly at the stick on the edge of the bath. Or more specifically at the word in the window.

Pregnant

That couldn't be right. It must be faulty. Thankfully, she had another two back up tests sitting on the kitchen counter.

But she couldn't make her legs move. There was no point. The test was right. She knew it was because she could remember how it had felt the last time. Only that time she hadn't known what it was she was feeling. It had been winter, cold and damp. She'd thought she was coming down with the flu and that was why she felt so heavy and exhausted.

She and Liam had gone to Chicago to see a band they loved, and it had been snowy. Liam had almost slipped over in the street, and she'd grabbed his arm. He had pulled away and she'd thought it was because he was embarrassed.

It wasn't that. Much later, when she had been torturing herself by replaying their relationship over and over again, she had realised that he hadn't wanted her to think that he needed her for anything. And she'd wished she could go back in time and let him fall on his backside. Or, better still, push him in front of a snow plough.

He had broken up with her by text, and even then he had lied to her.

I've met someone.

As if it had just happened when, in fact, he'd been married for two years. Was it any wonder then that when the cramps started, she had thought it was just her body going into shock?

They'd told her at the hospital. That she was pregnant but she was losing her baby. So, she had never done this part. This testing and watching the future emerge in a small white rectangle.

Back then, with Liam, she would have been thrilled. They'd talked about getting a place together. He'd sometimes teasingly called her 'wife'. They would have celebrated, cried, talked about names. Of course, none of that had meant anything. All of it, the talking about the future, the joking about marriage, had been lies designed to keep her hooked and stop her realising that he wasn't as invested in their relationship as she was. In reality, she'd always been on her own.

Just like now.

Only now she wasn't celebrating. She was terrified. Terrified at the thought of being a single mom. Terrified that this baby would be snatched away from her because she wasn't ready or happy or capable of being good enough. And she knew that she wasn't good enough. Just look at how unthinkingly she had got pregnant.

Worse than that, she'd done what she'd always striven to avoid doing. She had got pregnant by a man who didn't want her. The curse had come true. She was going to be another Fennell woman raising a baby alone.

Her body tensed as the buzzer to her apartment vibrated through the apartment, cutting across her panic. It was probably some food delivery guy dropping yet another pizza to her neighbour. But he'd work it out.

It buzzed again, loud and insistent. Whoever was pressing that buzzer was not going to give up, and, darting into her bedroom, she snatched up a pair of pyjama bottoms and pulled them on.

'Whatever it is, I didn't order it,' she snapped, yanking open the door. 'So, could you stop—'

Her voice died in her throat.

It wasn't a pizza delivery guy. It was Harris Carver.

She stared at him, her legs suddenly unsteady. Her lungs felt as if they were bruised on the inside. He couldn't know. Of course, he didn't. But what was he doing here? The panic she had been working so hard to stifle rose to her head in a rush and she stared at him mutely.

'You left your jacket at the office.'

He held it up, and after a moment she took it from his outstretched hand.

'Thank you. You didn't need to bring it round.'

'I wanted to check if you were all right. You left in a bit of a hurry and Cathy was worried about you. She said you'd had some kind of family emergency.'

Had she said that?

'Everything's fine.' She lifted her chin, smiled stiffly. She felt as if she were made of glass, that her skin was transparent and that she was open to him, just as she had been in that hotel room. Only that had been sex, and this was—

What was this?

The many, all equally unsettling answers to that question made her grip the edge of the door as if it were a cliff edge. 'I'm fine.'

Try telling that to your face, she thought as his gaze moved over her silk blouse and down to her striped pyjamas. She must look like a crazy person.

'It's nothing I can't handle.'

'You don't look like you're handling it.' Before she could stop him, he had taken her elbow and was gently guiding her back into the apartment.

'Sit down,' he ordered.

She sat, but then almost immediately got to her feet again as he turned and began striding away from her.

'What are you doing?'

'I'm getting you a glass of water.'

'I don't need one—' She reached out to grab his arm, but it was too late. He was already in the kitchen. There was still a chance he might not notice the boxes of spare tests—

But then she felt his sudden stillness. And it was how she imagined it would feel when a star collapsed in on itself in some giant, epic implosion. She knew without even needing to open her eyes that he had seen them, so she opened them anyway because choosing not to see something didn't stop it happening.

He was holding one of the boxes in his hand. His beautiful carved face looked like a bronze Emesa battle mask, and she felt her ribs snap tight as his grey gaze locked onto hers. She knew that she had gone pale, and that there was no way to hide that.

'You can't be pregnant. We used a condom.' There was a short, stifling silence as his gaze switched to the other boxes on the counter, then back to her face.

'Are you pregnant?' he said hoarsely. 'Have you done a test?'

She licked her lips, the directness of his questions making her sway a little as if his words were a series of jabs to her body. 'I've only done one and it could be wrong—'

Her voice faded, but then the look on his face was enough to rob anyone of speech.

'How pregnant are you?'

'I don't know. Six, maybe seven weeks.'

She could see him doing the maths. 'So, it could be mine?'

It? She swayed slightly as a rush of fury that was as fierce as it was unfair surged through her, but she didn't feel like being fair. She felt like weeping and hiding from this man who had already disassembled her poise and steadiness and was now barking questions at her like an inquisitor.

'If you mean *my* baby, that's none of your business.'

Which was a lie. It was very much his business. But earlier on today he had pretty much told her that she had nothing to do with his life. Obviously, she knew that was not a reason to hide the truth from him, and she would have told him at some point. But right now, she had hardly processed it herself and he was here wanting to call the shots just as if she were still working for him. But this baby wasn't some proposal that needed his signature.

'None of my business,' he repeated slowly and the tension in the room ratcheted up several notches.

'What?' She stared at him coolly, but given that she was dressed for work and sleep at the same time it seemed unlikely that she was pulling it off.

'We had sex once. We weren't exclusive,' she lied.

'You were sleeping with other people?' He seemed stunned.

'Oh, and you weren't.' Just thinking about him with some other woman made her feel wronged. Which sounded insane even in the privacy of her own head.

'Don't judge people by your own standards, Eden.'

'Maybe, don't judge, period, Harris,' she snapped

back. His name fizzed on her tongue like sherbet. 'What gives you the right to—'

'Fathers have rights too.'

Was that true? Panic stabbed her stomach. His voice was hard, all menace and that authority he wielded so casually in the office, but which felt terrifyingly out of place in this small apartment.

'Being there at the moment of conception doesn't make you a father except in the biological sense.'

'So, I am the father.' He moved then, leaning in, his hands pressing against the wall on either side of her.

'I didn't say that.' Being here with him was making her brain malfunction. She wanted him gone. Wanted to be alone so that she could process. But she also didn't want him to leave. There was something solid and reassuring about his presence and after last time—

She could remember it as easily as if it had happened yesterday. She hadn't understood what was happening. She had been alone and so scared—

She was still scared now, but at least she wasn't alone. Only she wasn't ready to deal with his reaction when she hadn't even come to terms with her own. And it wasn't fair of him to make this about himself. This was happening to her.

'You need to leave,' she said finally. 'I have a flight booked for San Antonio this evening, so I need to pack.'

He was looking at her as if she had grown a set of horns.

'I'm not going anywhere, and neither are you.'

'You're not my boss anymore. You can't tell me what to do.'

His face was harsh beneath the kitchen spotlights. 'I

can tell you this, I'm not going to be letting you out of my sight until I know for certain if that baby is mine or not.'

'What are you going to do? Put me under house arrest?'

He took a step back, but his hands were still on either side of her face, his arms and chest crowding her back against the wall.

'That's not a bad idea.'

'I was joking.' She felt a rush of panic. Could he make that happen? The whole thing was too ludicrous to contemplate but there was a tension to his body that made her think that, from his perspective, it was a definite possibility. 'You can't keep me locked up here for the next seven or eight months.'

'I won't need to. You can do a paternity test at seven weeks.'

She felt her stomach twist. A paternity test. This was all moving way too fast.

'But I just told you I'm only about six weeks pregnant.'

'Exactly.' His eyes snapped up to meet hers and he lifted his hands from the wall. 'Which means I need you to come with me and stay with me for at least a week.'

'No—' She was shaking her head, but he didn't even notice or most likely he had noticed but he didn't care.

'I'm not going to stay with you. I don't need to. I have an apartment. You're standing in it.'

'I'm not talking about staying in New York. You won't relax here, and you need to relax, and rest.' He assessed her face. 'You've been working flat out for weeks now and don't bother trying to tell me otherwise. I know how many hours you've put in, and that would take a toll on anyone. But you're pregnant. You need to take extra good care of yourself, and the baby.'

'I can take care of myself and my baby,' she began but he cut her off.

'But it would be much easier if you didn't have to think about anything else. I can make that happen. I have a villa in St Barth's. It's fully staffed, so you won't have to lift a finger. You can just lie by the pool for a week and then we can take the test.'

They didn't need to do one but, given that she had pretty much told him that she had slept with other people, he was hardly likely to believe that.

As for resting and relaxing, with Harris living under the same roof as her that seemed unlikely.

Her hands balled at her sides. He was glancing impatiently at his watch, and she desperately tried to think of an alternative to his crazy suggestion.

But then she remembered his knock on the door earlier. This was not a man who would give up or be open to persuasion. She would have to fight him, only she couldn't fight the way he did, as if it was all or nothing. Not even on a good day, and she was so tired and strung out right now.

How could that be good for the baby? Her lungs sucked inwards, scrabbling for breath. She felt not just tired now but sick with panic. She couldn't lose this baby too. Harris was right about her needing rest. Only that wouldn't happen here in New York. Or in San Antonio.

There would be too many questions to answer at home.

Maybe a week away in the sun might give her the space she needed and make him back off a little. It would be worth going if both those things happened.

'Fine,' she said stiffly. 'I'll come to St Barth's with you. For a week. Now, if you wouldn't mind, I need to shower and pack, so why don't you go sit in that nice, air-conditioned limo of yours and I'll be down when I'm ready?'

Without giving him a chance to respond, she turned and walked back into her bedroom, slamming the door behind her.

CHAPTER SIX

EDEN HAD KNOWN Harris was rich, but there was something about a private jet that made that fact screamingly obvious, and now she was more uncertain than ever that she was doing the right thing. Although it was a little late to worry about that, given that she was currently midway between New York and the Caribbean island of Saint Barthélemy.

She still wasn't entirely sure why she'd agreed to come with him other than she had simply run out of fight in the moment, and there was no obvious alternative. Getting him to leave would have been like trying to move a mountain.

She had been suddenly, brutally tired of it all. Not just the unreasonableness of his demands but the simple, ground-shaking shock of finding out that she was pregnant, because the last time that happened, she had already been losing the baby she hadn't even realised she was carrying.

The memory of those excruciating, agonising hours in the hospital made her fingers dig into the leather armrest. Through all of it she had been on her own.

Only she hadn't been alone earlier. And maybe that was the real reason she had agreed to go with Harris.

She glanced across the cabin to where he was working on his laptop. After she had reluctantly agreed to his plan, he hadn't left her apartment as she'd asked. Instead, he'd stood outside her bedroom like some watchdog while she'd jerkily packed a bag in silence. Then he had part guided, part escorted her downstairs to his car, which had sped them through the city to some private airfield and his waiting jet.

And that was that.

Maybe if she closed her eyes for a moment, everything would stop spinning long enough for her to be able to plan her next move.

'There's a bed.'

Her eyelashes snapped up like a roller blind. Harris was standing next to her, his grey gaze narrowed critically on her face as if she were a piece of modern art he wanted to understand.

'I hope you're not suggesting we use it.' It was a pointless, provocative thing to say but she had wanted to knock him off balance. Only now she felt off balance because she was thinking about the last time they'd shared a bed.

He ignored that, but a muscle twitched in his jaw, so he was likely thinking the same as her, which was something. 'You look exhausted. Instead of trying to sleep in your seat, you might like to lie down.'

She stared up at him warily. 'And where are you going to sleep?'

'I have some projects to sign off, so I'll be working for a couple of hours, and then I'll just sleep in my seat. But I'm not pregnant.'

His fingers pressed against the edge of her seat. 'Just

go and lie down, Eden.' He turned his head and one of the stewards appeared to accompany her to the other end of the cabin.

The bedroom was quiet, and the bed was surprisingly comfortable.

Stifling a yawn, she lay down, tucking her hand under the pillow.

'Oh, could you leave them open please?' she said as the steward started to draw the curtains.

'Of course, Ms Fennell. Is there anything else I can get you?'

'No, thank you.'

The night sky was different up here. There seemed to be fewer stars, but she wasn't looking for stars. She was looking for a single, bright white pinprick of light, and she was still looking when her eyelids closed five minutes later.

Tilting his head slightly to the left, Harris let his gaze track a yacht that was cutting a crisp white line through the brilliant blue sea. If that angle also allowed him to take in Eden's downturned face it was a coincidence, he told himself firmly.

They were eating a late breakfast out on the villa's deck. They had arrived in darkness and to lashing rain that was the tail end of a hurricane that was now heading to the mainland.

But this morning the sun was a brilliant Meyer lemon yellow, and the faded-denim-blue sky was cloudless. Better still, the forecast was for unseasonably placid weather so he would be able to make good on his promise to Eden of rest and relaxation beneath the Caribbean sun.

Although, truthfully, he didn't give a damn about the weather. All that mattered was that she was here. Not so much a prisoner as a hostage. As soon as he knew whether she was carrying his baby, she could leave. It wasn't exactly a chore, spending a week in the Caribbean. Most women would be delighted.

Eden was not.

He glanced over to where she was now staring pointedly out at the ocean. She was angry with him. But what gave her the right to be angry?

She wasn't the one who'd been left in the dark, because when exactly had she been planning on telling him she was pregnant? He had wanted to ask her that question multiple times already and he would if it turned out the baby was his.

And if it was?

He had asked himself that question multiple times too, and the answer changed each time. Except in one way. He would be a *major* part of his son or daughter's life. He would make sure of that, but he was getting ahead of himself. There was no point in spooking Eden by giving her advance warning of what he had in mind.

The last thing he needed was for her to disappear into the night as Jessie had, even though he fully understood why she had gone. Not turning up for the scan had sent her a clear message, or it must have seemed like that to Jessie, anyway. The truth was nothing had been clear. He had been floundering and scared and there had been nobody to ask what to do. He had felt so alone and ashamed and somehow responsible for having no one to go to. How could he be a father when he hadn't managed to be the son anyone wanted?

Pushing back against the tangled mess of emotions that thought provoked, he moved his plate to one side.

'Did you sleep well?'

Her eyes flashed to him then, the green of her irises vivid in the sunlight. 'Yes, it was very comfortable.' She hesitated. 'It's a very beautiful house.'

'I think so.' He had no reason to feel as pleased as he did by her somewhat reluctant approval. Maybe it was because she had offered it up uninvited, unlike the news about her pregnancy. 'I knew the previous owner and I asked him to let me know if he was in the market to sell and he called me two years ago.'

'Why this house in particular?' She had momentarily forgotten her anger and he wanted to keep her talking. Keep her looking at him like that as if she were genuinely interested in his answer, even though he knew it was just a hangover from their working relationship.

Relationship. The word jangled inside his head, and he was back to wondering about what would happen if he was the baby's father.

It would be different this time because *he* was different. When Jesse had told him she was pregnant, her assumption that he would marry her had made him feel as though he were drowning. She had been pretty and confident, and he had desired her in the moment, but he hadn't loved her, and she hadn't loved him. Just like his mom and dad hadn't loved each other. That mirroring of his parents' unhappiness had loomed large. So large that he hadn't been able to see past it.

By the time he'd realised what he'd done, she was gone, and his daughter was growing up with another man as her father. Picturing Jasmine's small, soft, trusting face, he felt his stomach knot. He had lost one child. He wasn't going to lose another.

He felt Eden's gaze on his face and, turning, he shrugged. 'Location, really. Saint Barthélemy is a beautiful island.' A true paradise on earth.

That wasn't the only reason.

Here in the Caribbean, the sky had the thinnest atmosphere, which meant the stars and planets were brighter and clearer. Explaining why that was important to him would reveal more than he was willing to share with anyone, but particularly the woman who might be pregnant with his child.

'And the villa is right at the tip of the island so the beach can't be accessed by anyone not staying at the villa. It's just you and me, and the staff, of course. I'll show you around. That way you'll know where everything is.'

'That's very kind of you but I'm sure I can get my bearings on my own. In fact, I might do that now.'

He waited until she was almost out of sight and then he got to his feet. He caught up with her easily, his longer legs making up the distance of her shorter strides. She turned, annoyed.

'I'm not going anywhere except the beach. So, unless there's some portal I can step through to get to London, you don't have to follow me around.'

'I was bringing you this.' He held out a sunhat and a tube of sunscreen. 'It's too hot for you to go bare-headed, and you need to protect your skin. Or I can do it for you,' he added as she stared at him in silence.

She snatched the hat and the suncream from his hand.

'I can do it myself.'

'Pity,' he said softly.

Her eyes fluttered up to his, looking startled.

'Why did you lie about where you were going?' he asked.

'I didn't. I am going to the beach.' She frowned, two lines creasing her forehead above her nose, and he felt a sudden almost unbearable urge to reach out and press his thumb into the grooves, then cup her cheek and pull her closer.

'I don't mean now. When I came to the apartment. I thought you said you were going to San Antonio so why did you say just now you'd go to London if you could?'

Her face stilled as if she'd just admitted to having a fake passport at border control, but then she recovered. 'London is further away from you.'

He sighed. 'This is going to be a long week if you keep on fighting me at every opportunity.'

'I didn't fight you. I gave in,' she said flatly. 'But if my being here bothers you that much, I'll happily leave.'

His jaw tightened. *Not happening*, he thought. Not until he knew for sure, and then—

He swore silently as his thoughts came full circle and he was back at the unanswerable question. Ignoring both it and her last remark, he took a step closer, holding her captive with his eyes, wishing he could do the same with his hands. Wishing he could touch her, hold her, press her close—

'Don't swim in the sea if you're on your own. You can paddle but if you want to swim, use the pool,' he said softly. 'Don't even think about climbing on the rocks. Put the hat on and use the sunscreen.'

'Don't you think that's a lot of rules for a twenty-five-year-old woman?'

'It's only four. For now.'

He turned and stalked away. 'Just don't break any of them, Eden,' he called over his shoulder. But only because he didn't trust himself not to stalk right back and kiss that disdainful curl of her mouth if he turned to look at her.

Eden.

She hated it when he called her that. But only because she loved how her name sounded in his mouth. He said it the way it was meant to sound, two soft vowels around a hard consonant. Hard and soft. Him and her.

As Harris's tall, muscular body disappeared from view, she turned and walked determinedly in the opposite direction.

Except there was no him and her. There was one night of amazing sex and a baby that was currently the size of a pomegranate seed.

Oh, wow—

Her footsteps faltered.

She was in paradise or at least the earthly version. Turning slowly on the spot, she let her gaze drift slowly over a perfect coalescence of the palest pink sand, brilliant blue sea and swaying green palm trees.

Without even realising she had done so, she had slipped off her sandals and scrunched up her toes in the warm, powder-soft sand, and some of the tension she had been carrying in her bones since walking into the club and seeing Harris waiting to interview her faded a little.

Actually, she had been tense before that. More than

tense. She had been rigid with misery and self-loathing and envy.

It was the week before she'd met Harris in that bar. She'd been getting ready to go out when Liam had got back in touch, and she had been shaking so much it looked as if the mirror were breaking apart. Or maybe that was her. It had certainly hurt that much. Hurt to move, to be alive.

She knew it wasn't just the shock of finding out that he had had a baby. That was a slap in the face but seeing Liam holding his son had stung for another reason, one that she had fought so long and hard to deny. Looking at a photo of her ex with his child was the closest she would get to having the family unit she coveted.

No wonder she'd still been spinning out when she'd walked into the bar. It was such a crushing reminder of who she was, who she had always been and could only ever be. To fight against that family curse would be a fruitless exercise, which was why she lived as she did. Why she had set up two offices on two different continents. Why she never met a man for a second date. Why she had taken Harris's hand but not asked his name.

Only then they had gone to that hotel room, and all the pain, shame and envy she had been feeling had melted away.

It was supposed to be just a night of passion with a stranger. Love, commitment, parenthood were not options. Except now they were. Somehow, that moment of ultimate pleasure had led her here to this beach.

She gazed out at the sea she couldn't swim in because she was alone.

He was right, she thought, glowering at the cool blue

water, resentment simmering inside her. This was going to be a long week.

But first she had to get through today.

Harris might have wanted her to be under his watchful eye, but he was perfectly happy to delegate the watching to someone else. One of the maids came to find her on the beach with a jug of chilled cucumber water, and every now and then as she wandered down the beach picking up shells, she would catch a glimpse of one of the security detail.

Harris did join her for lunch, briefly. But then, having reminded her that she needed to wear her hat and sunblock and adding in a new rule about staying hydrated, he murmured something about a conference call and disappeared.

After lunch, she was tempted to go for a long hatless walk, but the glaring heat of the afternoon sun defeated her, and she retreated into the villa.

Which was how she ended up standing in silence, staring at his shut office door.

He would never say it to her face, so he had let his door do the talking and the message was clear. She was useful as an employee and he was happy to share a bed with her for a night but other than that he had no interest in her.

That thought made her want to hammer loudly on the wood, and she was just lifting her hand when she heard his voice, followed by a deep laugh.

Her pulse accelerated sharply. She had never heard him laugh. But then their interactions to date had held few comic moments. Just raw, uncontrollable passion, angry accusations and some mutual cold-shouldering.

What would it take to make him laugh like that?

Nothing she had to offer, that was for sure. Even with Liam, when she had thought that theirs was an actual relationship rather than a side dish to one, they hadn't laughed much. Hadn't talked much either. Or argued. And at the time, she'd been so proud of herself, so convinced that it meant she'd found the yin to her yang.

Her fingers clenched at her sides. It was only later when she'd realised he didn't need to laugh or talk or argue with her because he could do all those things with his wife.

For Liam, she'd only ever been a thrill, a diversion.

And for the man on the other side of this door, she was just a baby carrier.

Inching backwards, she turned and walked softly away to continue her exploration of the villa. It was a lot more relaxing doing it on her own and without Harris's edgy, silvery gaze fixing on her face when she was least expecting it.

An hour later, she was hunched over a book she wasn't reading, trying not to watch him as he powered up and down the pool.

After New York's autumnal dampness, the blast of heat had knocked her out and she had decided to lie by the pool on what looked like a four-poster bed complete with sheer curtains that quivered in the whisper of a sea breeze.

She had been almost on the edge of dozing off and then Harris had emerged from the villa looking cool and composed.

And semi naked.

Okay, he was wearing swim shorts and flip-flops, but his chest and shoulders were bare and unadorned except for the flickering rays of sunlight that seemed to want to caress him as much as she did. She was still a woman, albeit a thwarted, pregnant one, and for a moment she let herself drink in his beauty.

Her breath stuttered in her throat as he pulled himself out of the pool, picked up his phone and began walking towards her. He stopped and squinted up at the sky, and she stared at the contoured muscles of his thighs and tried not to remember what it had felt like when they'd pressed against her bottom.

'What happened to the hat and suncream rule?' she said coolly, dragging her gaze away from his smooth, golden body.

He sat down beside her, and she had to snatch her feet back and tuck them under her legs to stop them from touching him.

'I'm used to it. And besides, I'm the boss. The rules don't apply to me.'

She glared at him. 'Let's just get one thing clear. You're not my boss. And I'm only following your rules because I choose to do so.'

'Or you like me giving you orders.' He turned his head slightly, staring at her steadily, his gaze soft but unyielding, and she felt suddenly unanchored.

'Do you mind?' She pushed his leg. 'You're getting water all over me.'

'Speaking of water, you don't seem to have any,' he said calmly as if she hadn't spoken.

'Then maybe you'd like to get me some. Please,' she added, handing him her empty glass.

He eyed her, then got to his feet, holding up his hand to stop the maid rushing forwards as he walked over to where a refreshing array of chilled water and juices and fresh fruit was laid out on a table.

Leaning back against the cushions, Eden tried to breathe normally but it was hard when Harris was still in view. Thankfully, his phone buzzed then, giving her a reason to look away. It was probably a notification about the space station. Did that mean you could see it from here? Would she be able to find it without his help? As much to distract herself from the sight of his back muscles as because she was curious, she picked up his phone.

She frowned.

It was a notification about Tiger McIntyre.

That was weird. Okay, McIntyre was a competitor, but that seemed a little obsessive, particularly as Harris played down their rivalry at every opportunity.

'Are you reading my messages?'

She glanced up. He was standing beside her, his grey eyes harsh in the sunlight.

'No. Well, yes, but only because I thought it was from the space station. Why are you getting notifications about Tiger McIntyre?'

'Because he's in the same industry as me and I want to know what he's doing.'

'But you have lots of competitors. Why follow him?'

'He's my biggest competitor, and I don't follow him.' But she got to her feet and chased Harris as he turned and walked inside.

'What is your problem with McIntyre? And don't play dumb because I know you know what I'm talking about.'

The tension in the room clicked up several notches. He was doing that staring thing he did so well.

'Okay. Don't tell me. But you know what, Harris, whatever he did, I'm starting to think you deserved it.'

'Then you'd be wrong. You don't know Tiger Mc-Intyre. You don't know what he did. What he's capable of.' He stopped abruptly as if he'd said too much.

'So, tell me? What did he do?'

'What does it matter to you? You're not saving my reputation now, Eden.'

Her breath stumbled as it always did whenever he used her first name. Which was why he'd done it, she realised a moment later. He was trying to knock her off her stride.

'It matters because, weirdly, I'd like to be able to think that the father of my child could be open and honest with me.'

'You want to talk to me about being open and honest?' The flare of incredulity in his voice made a shiver run down her spine. 'That's rich coming from you. I mean, when exactly were you planning on telling me you might be pregnant with my child?'

She hesitated. 'I don't know—'

He shook his head. 'In other words, you weren't going to. But given your lack of exclusivity, I suppose you thought the chances of my being the father of your baby were pretty remote.'

'That's not why I didn't tell you. I wasn't not going to.' That was too many negatives, wasn't it? 'I wasn't ready. I'd only just found out I was pregnant, and last time—'

Last time.

The words were out of her mouth before she even re-alised what she was saying and she felt all the air leave her lungs as she saw the look on his face—

She stepped past him, walking swiftly, blindly, back

through the house and up the stairs into her bedroom. Darting into the bathroom, she crouched over the toilet bowl, a visceral, twisting panic slopping heavily in her stomach like wet concrete, her fingers splaying protectively against her flat belly.

A flash of memory. Of a dull, throbbing pain doubling her up and blood, enough to scare her into a taxi to the nearest ER. The doctors and the nurses had been kind but brusque. But then it was an ER, and they'd been dealing with multiple casualties from a six-car pile-up on the freeway, so she had felt as though she were standing in the eye of a hurricane. They had asked questions she could barely answer and given her answers she hadn't been able to process and all the time she had been losing her baby.

Last time…

How could she have said that out loud? Might Harris not have heard her? Stupid question. She knew that he had. She had seen the expression on his face. Confusion. Shock, then understanding.

But he didn't really understand.

And she didn't want him to. She didn't need him to pretend that he cared. That he was interested in her. Yet it hurt to admit that. Just as it had hurt to admit that there was something off-key about her relationship with Liam.

The queasiness in her stomach was subsiding and she got to her feet and ran her hands under the tap to cool her wrists.

'Are you okay?'

Looking up, she flinched.

Harris.

Hovering outside the door, dressed now, looking not entirely sure of his reception.

'I'm fine.' He stepped back as she pushed past him. 'You don't need to check up on me.'

'But I do,' he said simply, and it sounded so genuine that for a moment she thought she might start crying.

'I don't want to fight you,' she said flatly.

'And I don't want you to give in.' He rubbed his jaw as if trying to erase something. 'I shouldn't have said what I did. I spoke out of turn—'

'Isn't that the point of being the boss? That it's always your turn—'

'But I'm not your boss. I didn't mean to upset you.' His jaw tensed. 'It's always like that. With him. With Tiger.' He stared past her, and she sensed that he was looking inside himself, seeing something there.

'So, you do know him.' A statement of fact, not a question.

He nodded. 'We were mates at college. For a time I was probably closer to him than anyone else on the planet. But then he slept with my girlfriend.'

She winced. No wonder he hadn't wanted to highlight his feud with McIntyre.

'How did you find out?'

His grey eyes snapped back to her, and he gave her a small, bitter smile. 'I wanted to talk to him about something and I saw her leaving his room. If they'd told me they wanted to hook up I would have been upset but finding out like that… I was so angry I wanted to hurt him.'

'What happened?'

'I punched him, he punched me back and we rolled around for a bit. It would probably have been okay, but

Tiger mouthed off to the dean and got kicked out. That was the last time I spoke to him. We see each other at industry events, and we go to the same parties, but we don't talk. I guess people notice that kind of thing and that's how the rumours started.'

He rubbed his jaw again.

'It was a stupid ego thing, which is why I've never talked about it. But I should have told you.'

'I understand why you didn't.' It wasn't fair that telling the truth made him look so solid and dependable then. Or that there was a softness to his eyes or maybe it was his mouth. Either way he was too close to her for it to be safe for him to look at her like that.

'I think I might have a nap,' she said, glancing pointedly at the door.

For a moment, she thought it had worked because he turned fractionally, his big body moving with that mix of precision and easy, masculine grace that had a gravitational pull all of its own. But then he stopped, and she fought down the desperation that was swelling inside her because she knew what he was going to say even before he said quietly, 'What did you mean, downstairs? About the last time?'

Harris watched her face stiffen. He knew what he'd heard, even though it was just two words. Last time.

Before he'd had a chance to fully absorb their implication, she was gone.

He'd stared after her, feeling every kind of terrible because he had hurt her. No, he corrected himself. He'd added hurt to her hurt.

Which was why he began moving, walking swiftly first to his room to change clothes and then to Eden's room.

The door had been open, which had spooked him as at first glance he'd thought it was empty, but then he'd seen her huddled over the toilet and he'd retreated, thinking she would rather him not see her like that. Only he hadn't been able to leave. His legs had simply ignored the messages from his brain.

Last time.

'Eden—' he said softly.

Her green eyes were wide like a child's. 'It doesn't matter.'

'It feels like it does,' he said carefully.

'It was a long time ago.'

He nodded as if he knew when it had happened, and what had happened.

'I've never been that regular with my periods so I didn't know.'

'You were pregnant.'

She nodded. 'Ten weeks. It was winter. I'd thought I was coming down with a virus and then I started getting these cramps. There was so much blood... I was on the way to the hospital, and I tried to call Liam, my boyfriend, but he didn't pick up and I didn't want to leave a message. I didn't want to panic him.' She made a noise like a laugh except it didn't sound as if she found it funny. He certainly didn't.

'I was scared, and I wanted him to be there, but then he texted me back.' Her voice was thick. 'He said that he'd met someone and that it was over.'

He stared at her in disbelief. 'Did you tell him what was happening?'

'I couldn't. He'd switched off his phone. I think he was scared how I'd react.' She pressed her hand against her mouth, and he wanted to find Liam and scare him as much or more than Eden had been scared.

'He texted me a couple of days after and I told him about the baby. He said...he said—' she breathed in sharply '—he said it was probably for the best. And it was for him because I found out later that he hadn't just met someone else. He was married.'

He could feel her shock and shame even now.

'I should have known.' Her voice was taut, as if she was having to break off each word to say it. 'It was so obvious, but I wanted to be different from my mom and all the other women in my family who pick lying, cheating losers. I wanted to prove that I had the good judgement they lacked, and that I could make a relationship work, so I just ignored all the signs. I didn't see anything, not even the fact that I was pregnant.'

She bit into her lip, hard. 'It was my fault. If I'd realised that I was pregnant—'

He reached out and pulled her against him. 'Miscarriages don't work like that, Eden. There's usually a reason they happen that is beyond our control.'

Her eyes found his, and he felt her fingers curl around his arm. 'I did want to tell you. That I was pregnant.'

'But you thought I'd react like he did.' He flattened his voice to make sure it didn't sound like an accusation, but she was already shaking her head.

'No, I didn't think that.' Her mouth quivered and there was a brightness to her eyes that made his throat burn with anger, and something softer, an urge to protect her and keep her safe from the men in the world who took and broke and wrecked without impunity.

'I was just scared of saying it out loud. Scared that something would happen to the baby.'

He pulled her closer. 'But nothing has.'

'It still might—' Her fingers tightened around his arm. He felt her fast breathing and he hated that she was so scared and that he had cornered her when she was so fragile but having to hide it.

It won't. He almost spoke the words out loud, but something in her face stopped him. The truth was that he couldn't say for sure that it would be all right, and she had been lied to enough by that bastard of an ex. Maybe he hadn't told her the whole truth about Tiger, but he couldn't lie to her about this. After being so bravely honest with him, she deserved honesty in return, and he wanted to give her that.

'It might,' he agreed finally. He spoke gently but firmly, projecting the calm neutrality that Eden needed right now. And that was the thing: even though they'd known one another only a matter of weeks and nothing between them was straightforward, he badly wanted to give her what she needed so that she would trust him and know that he was no Liam.

'But believe me when I say that I'll make every effort to ensure that doesn't happen.' Her grip loosened a fraction and he let his hand move to cup her head, feeling her soften against him. Despite the difference in their height, they fitted together easily, her curves accommodating his lines.

And on a purely selfish level it felt so good to hold her close.

His heart was pounding in his throat. Maybe she felt the same way, he thought as Eden looked up at him, and he allowed himself to let his hand slide through her hair and press her closer.

To let his lips brush against hers and taste her sweetness…

His breath hitched.

Her mouth was soft and warm, and he parted her lips, tasting her with his tongue, his stomach balling into a knot of heat as she leaned into him, deepening the kiss.

It would be so easy for his hands to roam over her skin, to nudge her back onto the bed.

He felt his body ripple to life. Easy and wrong.

He was not going to exploit her need for closeness and comfort to satisfy his needs, his desire. If it stung a little, so be it. He deserved it.

Gently, he loosened his grip. 'Why don't you get into bed and have that nap? If you want, I can stay up here. I have some more work to do.'

He hadn't planned to say that, but he was glad he did. She seemed to relax a little and five minutes after she slid under the covers, she was asleep. He could have left then, or he could have worked. But he did neither. Instead, he sat by her bed and watched her sleep.

It was something he'd never done. Something he'd never wanted to do. It was intimate on a different level and opened up a chasm of vulnerability he had never wanted to mine. But he couldn't leave. More accurately, he didn't want to. It felt right being here with her. There was nowhere else he could imagine being.

Not just then, but ever.

CHAPTER SEVEN

SHIFTING BACK ON his elbows against the sand, Harris tipped back his head and stared up at the black velvet of the sky, his gaze tracking the disappearing lights of a plane.

It was nearly one o'clock in the morning and it was a calm, cloudless night. Perfect for stargazing and he had already done a quick scan of the sky, ticking off the various stars and planets that were currently visible in this hemisphere. There was the Crux and Centaurus, and that was the Carina Nebula, a beautiful interstellar cloud that couldn't be seen in New York.

But he always came back to that bright speck of light.

Perhaps because of his navy training, or maybe it was just his natural reticence, but his father had never talked much about his working life. He had an office with the usual certificates and photos that men like him accumulated over their careers and even the odd souvenir of his time in space, but he'd never talked about his life up there.

Not with his son anyway. But then, out of all those photos, there was not one of his family.

Maybe that was why when his father had bothered to sit down one crisp winter evening and show Harris the light from the space station, it had stayed with him. Most days, when it was visible he would look up at least once during the evening to stare at it just as he had done when he was a kid.

Back then, those few minutes of gazing at that small but luminous pinprick of light had often felt like his only connection with his father.

It still did.

But there was another reason now that he kept up with his old habit. He liked to think that somewhere on the other side of the world, his daughter might be looking up at the brightest star in her sky and that her gaze and his would somehow meet in the middle.

Maybe she was looking right now. Looking for him.

Except he knew that she wasn't. Why would she be looking? She had a father.

It was a physical pain.

But at least she was alive.

He thought back to the moment when Eden had told him about her miscarriage and the pain in his chest made it hard to swallow. She had looked like a wounded animal, not just stricken but stunned, as if she were still there in the hospital losing her baby.

She had been so scared and alone and up in her bedroom it had been clear that she still felt that way now. He didn't know how to make it happen, but he knew he wanted that to change. He needed to do something so that she would feel safe, and know that she wasn't alone, that he would be there for her.

His pulse slowed as he remembered holding her close. She had felt right in his arms, so familiar, which made no sense because they hadn't even met six weeks ago.

Maybe it was because so much had happened in such a short time that it felt longer. It wasn't just the baby, it was the mess he'd made of his life trying to cage Tiger, and beneath it all an emptiness that seemed to mock his diary of prestigious invitations.

He had all this wealth and power. People hounded him to attend their events and yet he felt alone, just as if he were standing on the moon and gazing down at the Earth. But then he'd always felt alone even when he was theoretically part of a family. After his parents' divorce the feeling had been exacerbated but school had helped him lose sight of it. There you were rarely alone for long or given enough free time to dwell on how you were feeling.

By the time Jessie was pregnant and he'd found out he was going to be a father, he hadn't known how to let anyone get close.

And yet with Eden, it had been easy. Obviously, they'd had sex, so intimacy was a given.

Only it wasn't just about the sex. He'd felt a connection with her that went beyond bodies and damp skin and hands gripping each other tightly. Like in his office when he had shown her how to find the space station like some science geek. He'd wanted to see her reaction, to watch the way her green eyes danced with excitement when she spotted the light.

He had almost kissed her then. If Ted hadn't blundered in, he would have done.

He had wanted to kiss her yesterday after she'd told him about the miscarriage even though he'd known it would be reckless to do so. Kicking up the sparks from what had happened in New York would only complicate things and he hadn't wanted Eden thinking that was why he'd brought her here, because it wasn't.

Don't lie, he thought, his body loosening and tightening all at once. *You can lie to everyone else but not yourself.* Which was maybe why he had gone ahead and kissed her.

But she was here because until he knew if that was his baby she was carrying, she had to be.

His eyes lifted once more to the glittering stars. He wasn't going to lose another child. And to make sure that didn't happen he needed Eden to feel that her trust in him was not misplaced.

The following morning, she came down slightly late for breakfast.

He had expected… Actually, he didn't know what he'd expected, and perhaps that was a good thing. He'd made assumptions about Eden before and been wrong.

She met his gaze politely as she sat down opposite him and began to eat some of her fruit and home-made granola.

'About last—'

'I wanted to—'

They both spoke at once.

'You go first.'

She hesitated a moment. 'I just wanted to thank you for last night. I didn't mean to dump all that on you.'

'You didn't dump anything on me and there's nothing to thank me for,' he said slowly. 'I don't know how you've held it all together. Finding out you were pregnant and then me barging in on you when you were still stunned, press-ganging you into coming here.'

Remembering how he had frogmarched her to the waiting limo, he felt a hot wave of shame spill over him.

'It wasn't ideal. But if you hadn't turned up, I think I would have just stayed stunned. I needed to talk about what happened before.' Her green eyes were suddenly naked in a way that made him feel unhinged. 'That's why I got so upset yesterday. Saying it out loud for the first time. It was a bit of a shock.'

She'd never told anyone. But she'd told him. He stared down at her at the exact same moment she looked up at him and for a moment he could see himself reflected in the depths of her pupils. He knew that she must be seeing herself reflected in his and it felt so intimate and all-consuming that it took him an almost ludicrously long time to simply say, 'I can see that.'

'I know it must have been a shock to you too, but I wanted to tell you that you were very sweet, and kind.'

She hesitated then, and he waited, not wanting to probe or push; after all, he'd done enough of that already. Was that it? Was she including their kiss in his sweetness and kindness? Or did she not want to talk about that? His eyes flicked over her face, looking for clues.

Or maybe she just wanted to pretend it had never happened or almost not quite happened.

The latter, he thought, as she picked up her herbal tea and sipped it cautiously. She didn't say as much but he wasn't so lacking in empathy that he couldn't sense how little she wanted to have that particular conversation with him.

To distract himself from how intensely he wanted to know why that should be the case, he glanced over to where she was still sipping her tea.

'Is there something wrong?'

'No, it's just some things taste a bit odd at the moment, like coffee and regular tea, but this is fine.'

'Good.' He hesitated, feeling suddenly almost nervous. 'Look, I don't know how to put this, so I'm just going to come straight out and say it. I've arranged for us to see a doctor in St Martin this morning.'

'I don't understand.' Eden was staring at Harris in confusion.

'It's an island just a little further south from St Barth's. You might have seen it when we flew in,' he added. 'There's a private medical clinic there that I'm confident will be able to help us.'

'But it's too early. They can't tell yet—'

Frowning, he shook his head. 'It's not to do the paternity test.' He reached across the table and took her hand.

'I know you're worried about the baby, and I did some research and found out there's an early scan that can be done.'

The clinic in St Martin had a scanner that would be able to tell them what Eden needed to know right now. He would have preferred to use his own medical clinic in New York, and he had considered flying back, but it was the difference between a ten-minute hop in a helicopter and a four-hour flight and Eden was already stressed about the pregnancy. He didn't want to add to that stress.

'If you don't want to go,' he said quickly, 'that's fine. I just thought it might help.'

He felt a flicker of self-loathing because what had he done to help her so far?

Nothing.

His actions had been entirely self-serving, but he had

justified his behaviour in the moment because of what had happened in the past.

Except it was his past, not hers. Hers had been unknown, irrelevant. He had looked at her pale, stunned face and seen fear but assumed that she was scared of his reaction, never once thinking that she was terrified she might lose her baby.

He had put his own needs before hers.

But then what did he know about the needs of a pregnant woman? When Jessie had told him she was pregnant, his initial reaction had been a white-out of panic and disbelief followed by a string of swear words and a pinch of blame.

Unsurprisingly Jessie had seen him as another responsibility after that, rather than the support and confidant he could have been. He had never seen her again. She had left for Australia two days later and so, in answer to his own question, he knew nothing about the needs of a pregnant woman.

His jaw tightened. Out of all the many things he'd said and hadn't said that day, that pinch of blame was what he regretted the most. Thankfully, he hadn't done that with Eden, which was something at least. But he had coerced and chivvied her into doing what he wanted.

And he was going to have to live with that, as he was living with the consequences of letting Jessie down. But Eden didn't have to live with her fear. He could at least do something about that.

'It's called a reassurance scan. It's carried out between six to ten weeks. They can see the heartbeat and whether the pregnancy is the right size according to the date of your last period.'

Eden was still staring at him across the table.

'You did that for me?'

'The first proper scan isn't for another few weeks, but I know you're worried and the waiting is probably making it worse. I thought seeing the baby on screen might make you worry less.'

She smiled shakily. 'I think it will.'

It was already making her feel calmer, Eden thought as she walked back downstairs thirty minutes later to look for Harris. But it wasn't just the appointment. It was the fact that he had arranged it. That he wanted to help.

Which was astonishing given everything she had thrown at him yesterday. Most men would have been blindsided by what she had told him.

She had certainly blindsided herself.

Yesterday was the first time that she had properly allowed herself to go back there. To start at the beginning and push through to the end. At the start it had felt so real, not like a memory at all but as if it were happening all over again. She'd felt that gut-wrenching panic and desolation of losing the baby she hadn't had time to acknowledge.

Until Harris had pulled her close and she'd felt his warmth and strength seep through her, and her fear had subsided. Then it had felt real in a new way, a way she hadn't anticipated.

Finally, she had felt able to admit her grief out loud for the baby she had never met but whose absence she still felt so keenly. Harris had made that happen. Made the invisible visible. He had given shape to her loss, and she had never felt so complete, so seen.

And held.

Not shouldered like a burden that someone was waiting to put down, which was how Liam had made her feel. Harris had made her feel precious and necessary.

If she closed her eyes even a fraction, she could feel his body next to hers when he'd kissed her.

Her fingers twitched by her side as she remembered how his hand had splayed against her back for a second or two and how he'd inhaled deeply, breathing her in as if she were oxygen.

Standing there in his arms, she'd been lost in his heartbeat, completely at one with him to the point where she hadn't been able to feel where he ended, and she began.

And everything in the room, in the villa, on the island, on the planet had felt as if it had shrunk to the size of a pinprick, distant stars in the vast expanse of space.

There was just him.

Harris.

His mouth.

His pulse.

His breath.

The taste of him, and the heat of him.

The feel of his body tensing with pleasure as she'd leaned into him, deepening the kiss.

Her senses had exploded, body blooming, opening like a flower with the strength of her desire. She could have kept kissing him like that till the end of time. And she would have prised herself open or, better still, let him shuck her like an oyster.

But he had stopped it before they'd even got that far, and she should have been relieved. Things were already complicated enough between them. They didn't need to add another sexual encounter into the mix.

She knew that and yet she had felt hugely conflicted. More than conflicted, she had felt torn in two, and when he'd stepped away from her his absence had been like a physical ache.

'Ready?'

Harris was waiting for her at the bottom of the stairs. He looked casual and relaxed in cream chinos and a dark green polo shirt that emphasised the stretch of his biceps. Day-old stubble added to the whole 'billionaire on vacation' vibe, although there couldn't be many billionaires on the planet who were quite as temptingly louche and sexy...

'Yes.' She nodded firmly to try and shake her thoughts about Harris being sexy out of her head. 'Are we going by boat?'

He shook his head. 'We could take the boat, but it's quicker to fly. Not the jet, obviously. We'll take the helicopter. It's only around a twelve-minute flight.'

Of course he owned a helicopter. And there it was, squatting on a square of concrete like an oversized housefly. Except it was white, not black.

'Very chic,' she said quietly.

'Have you flown in a helicopter before?' he asked as he opened up the passenger door for her. 'Are you okay with this?' he added as she shook her head in answer to his first question.

'Yes, I'll be fine.' She frowned. 'Don't you want to sit in the front?'

'I will be.'

Her eyes moved over to the pilot's seat and then back

to where she was sitting. 'How? There's only two seats and the pilot's going to be sitting in that one.'

Harris nodded. 'He is. I am.'

Before she could react, he had closed the door. She watched him walk around the front of the helicopter and then he was climbing in beside her.

'You're the pilot?'

His mouth did that curving thing, which made the interior of the cockpit fade. 'I seem destined to constantly underwhelm you. Yes, today I am the pilot. Getting my licence was one of the first things I did after I had money to spare. I've been flying for about five years now.'

'I see.' Except she didn't. She just about managed to go to the gym twice a week. How on earth did anyone as busy as Harris have the time to learn how to fly a helicopter?

'You don't sound convinced.' He pressed a switch on the instrument panel.

'It's just I was remembering what you said about people not finding it easy to speak truth to power.'

He laughed. 'I wasn't talking about my helicopter instructor.'

She nodded but as soon as he'd laughed her brain had seemed to lose all functionality. All she could do was stare at him because she had got her wish. She had made him laugh and it felt undeniably good and a whole lot of other things that she couldn't give a name to.

Clearing her throat, she gave what she hoped was a casual, offhand shrug. 'Okay, then. But I think it's fair enough to have my doubts. I mean, I've watched enough movies where the hero has to fly something, and it all goes horribly wrong, and they have to use an inflatable dinghy for a parachute. What?' He was shaking his head. 'Is this where you tell me that helicopters are safer than cars?'

'Not right now. I'm too busy enjoying the fact that you see me as a hero.'

Her mouth felt suddenly dry. 'I didn't say that,' she protested.

He glanced over, his grey gaze resting steadily on her face, which felt hot and was probably tomato coloured.

'I was just…never mind…now could you please stop looking at me and watch the road or the sea or whatever it is that you have to watch?'

She had nothing to base her assessment on, given that she had never flown in a helicopter before, but Harris seemed to be as expert as he'd suggested. Occasionally, he would lean forward and press some button on the instrument panel. Once he pointed out a school of dolphins in the sea below and she had pressed her face against the glass, enchanted by the perfect synchronicity of their gleaming bodies as they leapt out of the water. Other than that, he was quiet and focused and exactly twelve minutes later the helicopter touched down on a different square of concrete.

A car was waiting for them, because that was how it worked in his world, and ten minutes later she was sitting on a couch in a pleasant, south-facing room at the Concordia Medical Centre.

Samantha, the sonographer, was very smiley and friendly but Eden could feel her body tensing as she waited. The last time she'd had a scan was after losing the baby. It had been a transvaginal scan with a probe that hadn't been painful but nor had it been particularly enjoyable.

'Do I need to undress?'

Samantha shook her head. 'No, not for this kind of scan. But if you could just pull up your top, Ms Fennell.'

She felt Harris shift forward in his seat. 'I don't have to stay if you—'

'I want you to,' she said quickly. 'If you want to stay.'

Their eyes met and he nodded, and the softness of his grey gaze and the size and solidity of his body made it easier to reach down and pull up her top.

'That's perfect, thank you.' Samantha smiled. 'Now, have either of you done this before?' As they both shook their heads, she gestured towards the window. 'Then you might be wondering why the blinds are closed. That's because it helps us to see the images more clearly. Now I'm going to put some gel on your skin and then I'm going to pass this probe over your tummy and a picture is going to appear on the screen.'

Eden glanced up at the monitor, her chest tightening. Please, she prayed silently. Please let everything be okay.

'And there is the baby.'

She breathed out shakily, relief churning inside her stomach. Harris's hand covered hers and she turned towards him and saw that he looked relieved too. Which made her feel guilty and yet oddly happy.

Samantha tapped the screen.

'So, everything looks good. First things first. I can see one baby. Heart is beating at around one hundred and forty per minute.'

Eden swallowed. 'That seems very fast.'

'Babies' hearts beat faster than ours.' Harris's deep voice seemed to fill the room as he spoke.

Samantha beamed at him. 'That's correct, Mr Carver. The foetal heartbeat is around twice as fast as an adult heart rate, so Baby Fennell is well within the normal range.' She moved the probe, then pointed at the screen. 'That's the umbilical cord, and I can see that the placenta is nice and high. As far as a due date is concerned, I could give you a rough estimate or if you're happy to wait then the twelve-week scan will be far more accurate.'

'I don't mind waiting.' Eden turned to him. 'Do you?'

He shook his head and she felt him squeeze her hand. 'I'm happy to wait.'

Samantha turned to type something into her notes. 'Obviously this scan is just showing us the baby's development at this time, but I hope you're both feeling reassured by what you've seen today.'

Eden nodded. 'I am, thank you.'

But it wasn't only the scan that had reassured her, it was Harris. The more she got to know him, the more she felt that she could trust him. That cool-eyed man with a list of demands who had pushed his way into her apartment was a hangover from the working day. Here, beneath the Caribbean sun, she was seeing a completely different side to him.

Softer. More approachable. A good man, a kind, decent man who would make a great father.

Which was more than she could have hoped for her baby, and that was all that mattered, wasn't it?

Yes, she told herself firmly. Okay, so there was something else between them other than the pregnancy. A heated shimmer that clung to the air around them, pressing in on them, pushing them closer, but that was just something left over from that night at the hotel. It would fade.

Samantha handed her some paper towels to wipe away the gel.

'I've asked Dr Krantz to step in, just to look over my notes, and if you have any questions, she'll be happy to answer them.'

Dr Krantz was older than Samantha but equally reassuring. 'I can see nothing of concern. Everything looks completely normal. So, keep doing what you're doing. Get plenty of rest. Keep active. Stay hydrated. I'm sure you're already following the guidelines when it comes to avoiding certain foods. If you're unsure, this booklet is very helpful.'

She handed it to Eden.

'I find that after experiencing a loss in pregnancy, many of my clients are often concerned about sex.' She glanced at each of them in turn. 'But unless there's been bleeding in the current pregnancy, which there hasn't, there's no reason to not have sex. Although you might be more comfortable trying out different positions. Now, any other questions? No? Then, I think we're all done. Except, would you like a photo of your scan? You can pick them up in Reception. There's just a small charge.'

On the flight home, neither of them spoke much. She was too busy looking at the photos of the baby, and Harris's attention was focused on the instrument panel. But as they walked back into the villa, she wondered whether he had been as focused as she thought because he still seemed oddly quiet and distracted.

She would give her right arm to know what he was thinking and feeling.

Her heart bumped against her ribs jerkily. Would he be feeling something different if he knew for sure that the baby was his? She felt a quiver of guilt that she had robbed him of that knowledge, and layered through that guilt was regret at her stupidity.

Why had she lied to him about having other partners?

But it was too late to do anything about that now. Once the paternity test had been confirmed then he would know exactly where he stood.

And then what?

It wasn't the first time she had asked herself that question, and she had assumed, hoped really, that time would bring greater clarity, but with every passing day she felt less sure of everything.

Other than that she liked him. A lot.

Best not to think about it too much, she thought, for the umpteenth time.

It was strange being back at the villa. She felt relieved, and then confused because it felt as if she had come home. But then it had been an oddly intimate morning.

What she needed was some time alone.

They had reached the top of the stairs, and she turned to face him. 'Thank you for arranging that. I feel a lot calmer now, but tired, so I might have a lie-down on my bed.'

'I might do the same. On my bed,' he added quickly. 'And I'm glad you feel easier about it now.'

As she made to move past him, their hands brushed, and his eyes locked with hers and she felt her stomach twist and tighten. They had been touching more today than any other day. In the clinic, he had taken her hand and then helped her off the couch and somehow, they had kept holding hands until Harris had broken his grip to shake hands with Dr Krantz.

This felt different though.

It felt charged. Expectant.

Harris was still staring at her, and then he looked down and seemed to remember that he could move his hand and he reached up to oh-so-casually rub the nape of his neck.

'Get some rest.'

He turned and walked away and she watched him for a couple of seconds before turning and walking in the other direction. The blinds had been left half down and her bedroom felt pleasantly cool. She sat down on the bed.

Rest.

She had told Harris she wanted to lie down, had thought she wanted to have some space, but his absence felt tangible and she had to curl her hands into the bed-spread to stop them from trembling.

Restless.

That was what she was. Her skin felt twitchy and too tight and just as it had when she'd walked into that bar all those weeks ago and seen Harris.

He'd scratched that itch in the way it'd needed to be scratched and then some.

She stood up and was moving out of the room before her brain caught up with her legs. Harris's door wasn't quite shut. Maybe if it had been, things might have turned out differently but, with her pulse racing and her mind clearly offline, it didn't seem like a big deal to just push it open a little further and walk straight in—

The room was empty.

Her stomach plummeted with disbelief and a disappointment that knocked the wind out of her so that she had to grab hold of the door frame.

'Eden—'

She blinked. Harris was standing in the doorway to what was probably his dressing room or bathroom. Or some other place where you might get undressed, because he had taken his shirt off.

He was staring at her, his expression pitched somewhere between shock and panic.

'Are you okay? Has something happened?'

Her heart folded in on itself because she loved that he cared. Loved that he cared enough not to hide his concern.

'Yes…no, I mean yes, I am okay and no, nothing's happened.'

Yet.

The word reverberated loudly inside her head, so loudly that she was surprised he didn't hear it. But maybe he did because now he was looking at her intently as if he might have misheard.

'You're not wearing a shirt.' Her gaze moved over his bare, muscled chest. The blinds were down lower in his room, but the sunlight loved touching him as much as she did and so a few stray rays were licking the curves and lines of his torso, gilding and illuminating them so that he looked like a painting by Caravaggio.

'I was getting changed. I thought I might go for a run.'

'In this heat?'

He cleared his throat. 'I can't seem to settle so I thought it might help.'

'I can't settle either. But I can't go for a run—'

He cleared his throat again, but his voice was still hoarse as he spoke. 'Perhaps something else might help.'

'Yes, I think it would.' She hesitated. 'I was thinking about what Dr Krantz said.'

His pupils widened and she knew that he wanted what she wanted, needed her as much as she needed him, and knowing that almost knocked the air out of her lungs. There was a moment of silence, a kind of charged stillness pulsing with possibilities. But really there was only one.

There had only ever been one.

They moved at the same time. He reached her first, pulling her against him with one hand and pushing the door shut with the other as he fitted his mouth to hers. Her fingers curled over his shoulders, scrabbling at the smooth, warm skin with relief and a hunger that was both rampant and infinite.

CHAPTER EIGHT

HARRIS COULD FEEL his pulse jerking in his throat. It was a clumsy kiss, urgent and inexpert, but it was all the more arousing for that.

She tasted so sweet, so hungry, and he was almost out of his mind with his need for her.

He pressed a kiss against her cheekbone, then her throat, then he opened her mouth with his tongue, deepening the kiss, tasting her, savouring her flavour—

His breath hitched as he thought about all the places he was going to kiss her. And lick her. He was going to lick that soft, pale skin until it gleamed like freshly poured cream and then he would lick inside her too.

He shuddered inside.

But first he needed to strip her, and, with his mouth still fused to hers, he reached for the hem of her T-shirt.

Eden moaned against his mouth, pulling away enough to make him growl an objection until he realised that she was tugging her top over her head.

He watched, his blood throbbing heavily through his limbs as she slid the straps of her bra down over her shoulders and he leaned in to lick her nipples.

Her hand fluttered against his arm, and he widened his mouth, sucking the swollen tip. She was gripping his arm now, fingers tightening as he licked and nipped and tongued first one then the other nipple.

A trembling warmth was creeping over his skin. He was so hard already—

Pulling back, he stared down at her, his heart raging in his chest, and then he found her mouth and parted her lips, kissing her hard, nudging her back towards the bed until she had no option but to teeter backwards and he had no option but to follow because their mouths were still fused.

They kissed hungrily and then he jerked backwards and pulled off her shorts and then dropped to his knees and pushed his face between her thighs, breathing in her scent, sensing the wetness beneath, stretching the cotton panties with his thumbs so that he could see the outline of her damp curls.

It felt indecent. Exquisite.

For a moment, he just stayed there, his hand gripping the bedspread, trying to steady himself, wanting to live in that moment, on the cusp for ever—

She arched then, pushing forward impatiently, and he hooked his thumbs under the waistband and slid her panties over her legs.

Now she was bare to him.

Soft. Wet. Warm. His.

He placed open-mouthed kisses up either thigh, feeling her tremble against his tongue, and then he parted her thighs gently with his hands, sliding the palms beneath the curves of her bottom, lifting her fractionally like an artist arranging a model, and then he lowered his mouth and licked.

She was slick, and blood-hot and so soft except her

clitoris, which was as taut and swollen as her nipples, and he wanted to keep tasting her for ever.

Her fingers were tight in his hair now, biting into the roots, the pain overlapping the pleasure he was feeling vicariously through her moans as she lifted herself against his mouth, rolling back and forth chasing the tip of his tongue.

He moved then, placing one hand on her hip bone just as he had done in the hotel all those weeks ago, anchoring her to him as he found her clitoris, grazing it with his incisors, sucking it fiercely into his mouth, then nipping it gently, then a little harder—

She swore then, breathing out the one-syllable word as if it had five syllables, and then she thrust forwards, body flexing against his mouth—

'Harris, Harris…' Her fingers twisted his hair as she pulled him onto the bed beside her.

Her fingers groped for his groin, clutching the front of his jeans as she felt the size of his erection.

'I want you inside me,' she breathed.

'Are you sure that—'

'Dr Krantz said it would be okay.' She was panting, pushing him back against the bed, reaching for his zip.

'Eden—' His voice was ragged, her name becoming a groan as she managed to free him, her fingers moving lightly, almost reverentially to trace the veins beneath the velvet-smooth skin. Exhaling sharply, he snatched her wrist as she straddled him.

'I can control the depth this way…'

Good, he thought, because he couldn't control anything.

She was lowering herself down onto the tip of his erection, and it was her turn to set the pace, dipping back and forth, curving herself in a way that he felt everywhere.

'Like that, like that,' he chanted, swearing under his breath as she dipped again because this time she stayed low, then pushed lower still and stopped. The feel of her stretching around him was almost enough to tip him over the edge and now he was panting too, his breath scraping up through his throat in time to the rocking motion of her hips.

His hands moved to clamp her waist and he rocked against where she was so warm and pliant, lifting her slightly so that he could withdraw and brush the blunt head against her clitoris, and he could hardly breathe through what was undoubtedly the most potent pleasure he'd ever experienced.

She made a choking sound as she slid down onto him again and he came, quicker than expected, hotter and harder than he'd ever come before, his body spilling inside her, his mind wiped clean of everything except the rightness of it all.

She was shaking, he was too, or at least his arms were and, gently, he lifted her up and instantly had to stifle the yelp that rose in his throat because it felt as though he'd been cut adrift like an astronaut floating off into space. He tipped her gently to one side and she slithered onto the mattress, her warm breath shuddering on his chest as he scooped her against him.

'Eden...'

He pulled her closer, sliding his leg between her thighs so that he could feel her wetness and his combined.

She was his, he thought, pulling her closer, his mouth seeking hers, then dropping to the pulse raging in her throat and licking a line back to her mouth, his hand sliding over to where their sweat was pooling on her still-flat belly.

Always his.

Eden woke with a jerk to darkness. Every day since that first time with Harris she had woken abruptly, feeling lost, displaced, confused. Not today. Today she knew exactly where she was even though this was a strange bed.

She knew because Harris was here too, lying beside her, breathing softly, his arm draped across her waist, tethering her to him. They could never be strangers. Had never been strangers, she thought, remembering how she had felt the morning after in the hotel. It had been so hard to leave him because it was like trying to separate herself from her shadow.

Or her soul.

Unnerved by the unfamiliar poetry of her thinking, she shifted position, turning away from the beautiful man who had dominated her thoughts ever since that night in the bar and now felt like a fixed presence in her life.

Like the moon.

She stared up at where it sat in the inky night sky, pale and serene and unchanged from when she had stared up at it as a little girl who dreamed of finding, not a prince, but a man with integrity and stamina and strength of character.

Liam had acted like that man. But he was a charlatan. A snake oil salesman.

Harris was everything that Liam was not.

Her cheeks stung suddenly.

What must the villa staff have thought? They had

spent the rest of the day in bed. Although Harris must have got up at one point and gone downstairs because when she'd woken up in the early afternoon, there had been a tray of food waiting for her.

He had brought cutlery and napkins too, but they had been like survivors of a storm. She hadn't even bothered to thank him. She had just started to eat, picking up pieces of fried chicken with her fingers. And he'd watched her, making sure she had some of everything before he'd started to eat. Looking out for her. Taking care of her.

She felt blissfully relaxed, as if every piece of tension had been smoothed flat by a hot iron. Unsurprisingly, given that the first time she'd ridden him to a shuddering climax had been just the beginning. And after each subsequent time, he would pull her close, and she would collapse against him, her body spent and limp and her muscles inside fluttering like a kaleidoscope of butterflies.

That was a good description, she thought, her hand moving lightly over the muscles of his chest. She had read about people who experienced life in colours— synaesthesia, that was what it was called. It was when two senses merged into one. Sex with Harris was like being at the centre of an opal. It was not just a physical act but a metaphysical one.

An act of love.

She stiffened against the mattress, panic stealing the breath from her lungs.

No, she wasn't looking for love. In fact, she was actively avoiding it. Avoiding anything that might lead her down that self-destructive path. Liam had cured her of thinking that was ever an option for her and, even if a part of her dreaded becoming yet another Fennell woman raising a baby on her own, it would be different with Harris.

They might not be together, but she wouldn't be on her own. He was already more involved than her father had been at this stage. Look at how quickly he had arranged the scan, and earlier he had made sure she ate.

She felt a pang of guilt, remembering his expression of relief when he'd seen the baby alive and well on the screen. Had he known for sure it was his, then he would have been able to fully express his excitement. They could have been excited together.

If only she hadn't panicked when he'd turned up at her apartment. But if she had told him that he was the father, would he have taken her word for it? It seemed unlikely. The paternity test would give him the certainty he needed, and, for the first time since she had found out she was pregnant, she wished she could bring the date forward.

'Eden—'

She blinked as Harris's voice cut across her thoughts. Moments earlier, his eyes had been closed, but now he was rolling onto his elbow and looking down at her, his grey eyes silver in the moonlight.

'Are you okay?'

'I was looking at the moon.' But it was forgotten now; its gravitational pull had nothing on Harris, and, clutching blindly at his muscled arm, she leaned into him, feeling her body soften and open for him once more.

'I thought we might go down to the beach this morning. We can take a swim and then I could show you the rock pools.'

Eden glanced over at Harris. They had spent almost every minute of the last few days together, so it was easy for her to press her hands to her mouth and mime shock. 'I thought the sea and the rocks were off-limits. Aren't you breaking your own rules, Mr Carver?'

He caught her ankle and tugged her towards him gently beneath the table so that her chair scraped against the decking. 'I prefer to see it as unmaking them.'

She raised an eyebrow, her green eyes dancing in the sunlight. 'In other words, there's one rule for you and one rule for everyone else.'

'I'm the boss, remember? There are no rules for me.'

'But you haven't always been the boss,' she said after a moment, still teasing him.

Not as a child, no. Then he'd been powerless to change anything in his life. He'd been as small and irrelevant as a pawn on a chessboard. And that feeling had got worse after the divorce, because both his mother and his father had been so eager to pursue the life they'd each wanted without the other that he had been forgotten in the rush to move on.

Which was probably why becoming wealthy and powerful had felt so good, feeling stronger and more authoritative than everyone around him. He hadn't misused his power. He wasn't a bully but for the first time in his life he was in control. He felt safe being the boss, and staying safe meant keeping his life free of anything random or spontaneous.

His thumb twitched against the skin of Eden's ankle.

Like picking up a beautiful stranger in a bar and renting a hotel room for a night.

And yet he couldn't regret that night. He didn't regret it.

He couldn't even completely regret turning up at her apartment because it had brought them both to this island. Brought Eden into his bed.

If he had a regret, it was that he'd not woken first that morning at the hotel. Had he done so, he would have made it clear to her that he wanted it to be exclusive between them.

The idea of another man being with Eden, doing what he had done, touching her, caressing her, opening her body to his, made him want to smash things. He had never felt that way about any woman before. So possessive, so proprietorial. So jealous. Not even with Franny, his ex, the woman he'd got into a physical fight over with Tiger.

But then, despite what he'd said at the time, that fight had been as much about Tiger's betrayal as hers.

More, in fact, because he hadn't loved Franny.

And yet when he thought about it now, it all seemed so long ago, and it was hard to see why it had felt so important.

Why did it matter if Tiger had hooked up with one of his exes a decade ago? As for Franny, maybe she had sensed that his heart wasn't in it. Which, he could see now, was a betrayal of a different kind.

He glanced across the table. Eden had been hurt a lot, and betrayed too in the most devastating way, but she hadn't gone after Liam with the sole, precise purpose of ruining his life. Nor had she risked everything she'd worked so hard to build simply to prove to the world once and for all that she was the bigger and better person.

Even though she was.

She was certainly a far better person than him. He thought back to the moment when she'd thanked him for taking her to the scan. How would she feel about him if she knew he had a daughter living on the other side of the world? A daughter whose scan he hadn't attended. He hadn't been there for her birth. Or her first steps. Or her first day at school.

'I haven't always been the boss, no. And I'm not your boss, Eden,' he said softly. He gave her ankle one last caress, then released her. 'In fact, I'm in awe of you.'

Her eyes found his. 'I thought you wanted me to be subservient to you.'

His body tensed, and it took a second, several actually, before he could speak. 'Two things can be true at once.'

'Schrödinger's cat, you mean.' She held his gaze and then abruptly got to her feet. 'I think they can. But maybe we should test that theory. And keep testing it until we know for sure.'

They made it down to the beach after lunch for the promised expedition to the rock pools. From a distance they looked empty but up close they were home to a surprising amount of sea creatures.

'It's even more crowded than New York,' she said, leaning over to peer at the underside of a rock that was covered in spiny sea urchins. 'Although it's a lot quieter.'

'Do you mind the quiet?' he asked curiously.

'Of course not. Quiet is how I measure my success, remember?'

His heart stumbled as she smiled. 'Or perhaps you were too busy gunning for me to listen to what I was saying.'

'Gunning for you?'

'That first interview. With Avery. You were so furious with me—'

'It was more the situation.' He stopped as she rolled her eyes. 'Okay, yes, I was furious with you. And with myself for not reading up on who I was meeting.' *Because I was too busy thinking about you*, he thought. Busy and bereft too. As if he had misplaced something precious. 'For a moment I thought I was dreaming and that any moment I was going to start falling out of an airplane—'

She laughed. 'In my dreams I feel like my teeth have fallen out. Or that I'm naked.'

'I wish I was in your dreams,' he said softly and as her eyes met his, he thought he had never felt more rooted in the reality of his body, and his need for her.

Ducking her chin, she lowered her gaze back to the water. 'Why do you think they're called urchins? It seems such an odd name. I thought it meant some scruffy child.'

'It comes from an old Latin word that means hedgehog, which was what they used to be called, I believe.'

'Sea hedgehogs.'

'Exactly.' He nodded. 'What?'

'Nothing.' She was staring at him, curious and a little confused and perhaps also with something that bizarrely felt like delight. 'I thought you were an engineer, not a biologist.'

He pulled her closer. 'I'm very interested in biology.'

It was a beautiful afternoon. The sky was cloudless and there was a light breeze that made the water dance and shimmer. Not that he cared. Frankly he could have been standing in the middle of a desert. He only had eyes for Eden. The sight of her in a bikini made it almost impossible to keep his hands off her. So, he didn't.

And she was as eager to touch him.

'I think it must be my hormones.'

'Are you saying I could be any man?' Sweeping aside the swathe of dark, glossy hair, he leaned in and kissed her throat, licking the salt of her skin, his body hardening as he felt shivers of anticipation ripple through her body.

'Well, any billionaire with a villa on a Caribbean island and a private jet and a helicopter— Ouch!'

She twisted out of his arms as he nipped the apple tattoo on her shoulder, but then leaned back into him almost immediately, pressing the curve of her bottom against his already hardening erection.

'He doesn't exist. I'm the only one.'

'My one and only.' She fluttered her eyelashes at him, biting into the smile curving her mouth.

Yes, he thought, gazing down at her mutely, except looking wasn't enough. It rarely was, he found, and he pulled her closer, wrapping his arms around her waist. Fitting his mouth to hers, he kissed her fiercely.

He'd never been one for love bites or tattoos, but he wished there were some way he could mark Eden as his.

'If you keep touching me like that we're going to have to go back to the villa,' she said, her voice husky, her hand curling over his to flatten it against her body in a way that knocked the air out of his lungs.

'Why? It's a private beach.'

'Not that private.' Shielding her eyes, she tilted her head back and he followed her gaze across the water to where a yacht had dropped anchor. She cut a glance in his direction. 'Do you have one of those too?'

'Yes. Mine's a lot bigger.'

'Is that what you say to all the women you bring here?'

She was teasing him, but he shook his head. 'I've never brought anyone here,' he said, surprising them both because he could never be accused of oversharing. But Eden had told him so much about herself and her life and all he had given her in return were some half-truths about his relationship with Tiger.

'This place is just for me. And you,' he added softly.

For a split second, her eyes were naked to him, and he watched a series of emotions flicker in the green irises.

'As for the yacht, I mostly use it for business meetings.' He grimaced. 'I know that must sound crazy, but it makes a lot of sense for people like me who work in sensitive industries. It means we can talk freely away from prying eyes.'

'I can understand that. At least they're not photographers.' She turned to him, biting her lip. 'Or could they be?'

He shook his head. 'No, they'd be snapping away by now. They don't hold back. Particularly if there's a beautiful woman in a bikini on show.'

A flush of pink seeped into her cheeks. 'I think they prefer their women in bikinis to be more glossy and less unkempt.'

'Glossy is fake. Your beauty is natural. Untouched. Except by me,' he said, leaning in to brush his cheek against hers. He meant every word. Without make-up and with her hair loose and grains of sand sticking to her skin, Eden looked like some Girl Friday and her beauty was all the purer for it.

He had kept his hand around her waist, but his thumb

was stroking the smooth skin there as if she were a piece of fruit he was testing for ripeness.

He could think of other, better tests only they would involve nudity and more privacy than the beach was currently offering, and he glared at the yacht, tamping down his irritation at not being able to take Eden in his arms again. 'I suppose you're right. Al fresco sex on a beach in front of a bunch of day trippers might not be the most sensible course of action for someone with a reputation crisis.'

She frowned at him. 'Former reputation crisis, you mean—which reminds me… I might just have a quick browse online. Can I borrow your phone? What? It'll take two minutes and it will help me relax.'

'Fine. Two minutes and then we go back to the villa.'

Rolling over, he grabbed his phone. He felt weirdly jealous and annoyed that he was having to compete with himself for Eden's attention.

'Here.'

He watched her type in his name.

'What the—'

She was staring at the phone as if it had turned into a snake.

'What is it?' His hand stiffened against the sand. 'What are they saying?'

'It's not about you. It's Tiger McIntyre. He's engaged!'

He waited for anger to swell against his ribs, but he felt nothing, except curiosity.

'Really? I never had him down as the marrying type. Who is she? I hope she's smart enough to keep him interested—'

'She's a white hat hacker, whatever that is, so I guess she'll keep him on his toes.'

There was a knot in his throat that made it hard to breathe.

'A hacker?'

Eden nodded. 'Her name's Sydney Truitt— What is it? What's the matter?'

She was looking at him, her face still, frozen with something that was on the way to confusion, and he knew why, knew that the shock, the utter disbelief, maybe even the panic he was feeling must be completely visible on his face. But he didn't know how to hide it, because she had made him soften, made him open a crack, and he was angry with her for doing that to him, and angry with himself for letting her, and so when he replied, his voice was taut and defensive.

'Nothing.' The lie stung. He didn't want to lie, and he couldn't look at her while he did so he glanced away, fixing his gaze on the yacht. 'I'm just surprised Tiger's settling down.'

Eden was still staring at him, and, slowly, she shook her head. 'But you weren't.' Her green eyes roamed over his face. 'Not really. Not when I first told you. You were just interested—'

'So, I had a delayed reaction.'

'But that's my point. You didn't react. Not until I told you about Sydney.'

This time he managed to keep his voice level when he heard the name. 'You don't need to monitor my responses any more, Eden. Your contract ended days ago.'

'Do you know her?' The bluntness of her question made him blink. But the answer would be too exposing.

'No.' He shook his head, the lie vibrating inside him and there was nowhere to look where it wouldn't still be a lie. 'I've never met her.'

At the shoreline, tiny waves were rippling over the sand, then withdrawing to leave it spotless. If only he could rewrite his past as easily. Beside him, Eden shifted position, and his palms itched to touch her again but there was something brittle about her posture, as if touching her might cause her to break apart.

'That's a little baffling,' she said flatly. 'You see, this article has a quote from Sydney Truitt saying that it was you who introduced her to Tiger.'

'Eden—'

'How do you know her?' She cut him off. 'And don't tell me she's lying.'

'She's not lying. But she's certainly twisting things.'

'Why would she do that?' She breathed in sharply as if he'd upended a bucket of cold water over her. 'Did you sleep with her?'

'No.' He shook his head vehemently. 'She worked for me, okay? Just briefly. I only met her once—'

'Then why is she saying you introduced her to Tiger McIntyre? Why would you even do that? You hate him. You told me you hadn't spoken to him for years.'

'I haven't and I didn't introduce them.' He hesitated, because in a way he had. 'Not directly—'

'Then why...why would she—'

Her voice faltered and he saw it first in her beautiful green eyes, her brain stumbling over the truth, the dawning realisation of what she was looking at, of what he had done.

'She's the hacker, isn't she? She's the one you paid to hack McIntyre's server.'

He stared down at her, watching an overlapping slide-show of emotions cross her face it, and the incongruity of their swimsuits seemed to highlight the cruelty of his simple, 'Yes.'

But he couldn't lie to her when she was looking at him like that. As though she was struggling to breathe.

She flinched, her green eyes widening, and abruptly the slideshow stopped, settling on anguish. His heart felt as if it were splitting in two. He had never felt so wretched or so alone.

'Eden—'

'Don't.' She was getting jerkily to her feet. 'Whatever it is you're going to say, don't bother.'

'I can explain—' He was standing now, moving closer, holding up his hands because he needed her to stay, to listen, to understand.

'I'm sure you can.' She was inching back from him as if he were a rattlesnake. 'Men like you always have an explanation for everything, and it's always so believable, so eloquent. But I don't need to hear any more lies.'

'I'm not going to lie to you.'

She was moving now, her stride clumsy and uneven as she walked.

'You know, funnily enough, that doesn't carry much weight right now, Harris. Because you are a liar. A compulsive liar. You don't even know you're doing it, or maybe you do, and you just don't care—'

'I do care. But you have to understand, he stole from me, and I was trying to prove that.'

'What about Avery? Does she know?'

'No, she doesn't know anything about it. None of the C suite do. I met Sydney on my own. I know, it was stupid, but when I heard about the prototype of the drill that was exactly like ours, I was so furious with him.'

'So, you lied to Avery too.'

'I didn't lie, I just didn't tell her about it because—'

'Because you knew it was wrong. And they would have stopped you.'

'Yes. But they didn't need to find out.' He hated how she was looking at him. As if she was seeing him for who he really was. 'Look, Tiger plays dirty. If he wanted to shaft me, he wouldn't do it obliquely. He's warning me off, but that's all it is, a warning. It doesn't matter.'

He reached for her wrist, but she didn't seem to notice.

'It does matter. It matters to me.' Her green eyes slammed into him. 'You know, weeks ago I asked you if there was anything I should know, anything that might come out, and you never said a word. Not then, not afterwards. And I stood beside you. But what if this comes out?'

They were back at the villa and now she seemed to notice his hand on her wrist, and she began to tug at it. 'I'll look like a fool. My career will be over.'

He tried to pull her closer.

'That's not going to happen. I would never let that happen to you.'

Eden hadn't felt nauseous for days but now she felt sick again. He made everything sound so plausible. Made her believe in him. Because, just like the last time, she had wanted to believe.

'Forgive me if I don't take your word at face value,

Mr Carver.' She glanced up the beach. 'I can't do this. I can't be here. With you. With someone who lies and thinks that it doesn't matter.' Her hand moved protectively over her stomach. 'I thought you were a good person. I thought you were different, but you're not. You're a liar. But guess what?' She gave a mirthless laugh. 'So am I. I didn't sleep with anyone else. I said that because I was angry with you, and scared. But I wish I had.'

'Don't say that—'

'Why not? It's true. You don't deserve to be a father.'

His face stilled. She had wanted to hurt him like he was hurting her, but she had assumed he would react, deny her words or tell her that she was a hypocrite as well as a liar. But he said nothing. He just stared at her, an expression on his face that she didn't understand because it didn't make sense. He looked stricken.

Haunted.

'Yes, you're right. I don't. I'm just grateful it took you this long to work that out,' he said slowly. 'If you want to leave, I won't stop you. Use the jet.' There was a strange brightness to his eyes now and, for a moment, he hesitated as if he was going to say something else, but then he sidestepped past her and walked back down the beach.

CHAPTER NINE

SHE STARED AFTER HIM, a stone sinking heavily in her stomach.

He was in the wrong.

He had lied to her.

To Avery.

To the world.

He had jeopardised his reputation, again. And hers.

He was bad news. Literally.

But none of that seemed to matter. All she could think about was that look on his face.

Thanks to its proximity to the equator, the sun was already starting to sink. The first few days in St Barth's it had surprised her that the evening light disappeared sooner than in New York.

Now it filled her with panic. Not like in the apartment when she'd found out she was pregnant. This was the wordless, slippery kind that made thinking impossible. She'd felt it at the hospital when her world had expanded and then devastatingly contracted in front of her eyes.

There was nothing she could have done differently to keep the baby. She knew that now. Or rather, thanks to Harris, she had accepted it.

And in accepting it, she understood the difference

between having a say in the outcome of something and having no choice. Here, now, she had a choice, and she was choosing to go after him. She had left a linen shirt of his that she was using as a cover-up by the pool, and she slipped it over her bikini, and then ran lightly down the steps to the beach.

She walked swiftly along the shoreline using the reflection of the moonlight on the water to find her way. She had expected to find him quite quickly, but it was a good ten minutes before she saw him sitting on the sand, his gaze fixed on the stars.

She felt suddenly fragile and untested. In his room, on his bed, she felt strong and sexy and insightful. She knew instinctively how he liked to be touched. Knew that if she caressed the flat of his stomach, his breath would go shallow, and he would grab her wrist as if he wasn't quite in control of his body's responses.

She loved the power he let her take in those moments. Loved giving power to him too. Being subservient to each other's needs was not just an aphrodisiac, it was a shared moment of vulnerability, and responsibility when they revealed and unlocked themselves.

Only looking at him now, she felt that confidence falter. He looked barricaded and yet desolate and, until recently, she'd had so little experience of addressing her own demons, was it likely she would be able to help him face his?

But she had to try. It was as simple as that.

So, in the spirit of that simplicity, she walked up and sat down beside him. He didn't react. Didn't acknowledge her in any way but she felt his body tighten.

'When I went to the hospital, they were kind about it

but when they told me that I was…' she frowned '…that I had been pregnant, I could tell they were surprised I didn't know. Because I was a college graduate with a job and a partner. I felt so stupid. Not just about the baby, but about Liam, and I felt like I was being punished for my stupidity. I felt like the worst person in the world. The worst mother,' she said slowly. 'But I wasn't to blame. I didn't deserve to lose my baby—'

'Of course not.'

He spoke now as she'd hoped he would, his arm brushing against her leg as he twisted towards her. 'You didn't deserve that lying jerk of a boyfriend either.' Against the pale sand, his profile looked bleak suddenly. 'But then I'm no better.'

He turned away, or tried to, but she reached for his arm, curling her fingers around his elbow.

'I can assure you, you are. And I'm not the only person to think so. Avery thinks you walk on water. All your staff do. And no, I didn't ask them. I eavesdropped in the restroom and in the elevator and I didn't hear one bad word about you. You're a good person who did a bad thing but you're not a bad person.'

Hunching his shoulders, he shook his head. 'You only think that because you don't know what else I did.'

'You mean the details?'

'I'm not talking about the hacking.' He ran his hands over his face, pressing the palms hard against the temples as if he wanted to crush his head to a pulp.

'Harris, don't.' She moved to kneel in front of him, reaching for his hands.

'It's not just the baby I don't deserve,' he said tiredly. 'I don't deserve you. I don't even know why you're here.'

'I'm here because you're not the only one who lied, remember? I did, back in New York. I told you I'd had other partners. But I didn't. There was only you.'

My one and only, she thought, replaying the moment when they had been teasing each other earlier.

'Which makes you the father of this baby.'

'Which is the reason you should leave.' His voice was barely a whisper now. 'I don't have what it takes to be a father. If you don't believe me, ask Jasmine.'

The silence that followed that statement seemed at home with the darkening sky and the stars. But Harris was staring at them as if they were a judge and jury combined.

'Who's Jasmine?' she said softly.

He didn't answer immediately but she could feel him sifting words inside his head, stacking up sentences then abandoning them just as she had done so many times when she'd tried telling someone about her miscarriage. Which was why she let the silence stretch because this had to be on his terms. If he wanted to go through every word in the dictionary she would wait.

'She's my daughter.'

A daughter. Her head snapped up.

Harris had a daughter.

He was still gazing up at the sky but there was a tightening around his mouth, and she knew that all of his senses were tuned into her reaction. She was shocked and yet part of her wasn't. A part of her felt as if she had always known. Maybe it was the way he'd reacted to her pregnancy. He had been so focused and yet also on edge. Not because she might be pregnant with his child but because she might not be.

Harris was silent again, and again she waited, because that sentence and all that it implied deserved to be absorbed and acknowledged without some rushed and intrusive questioning on her part.

'She could tell you exactly what kind of father I am because she's never met me. Never spoken to me. I don't even know if she knows what I look like.'

'How old is she?'

'She's eleven.'

'Where is she?'

'Tasmania. She lives there with her mother.' A pause. 'And her stepfather.'

His voice was calmer now, but there was an ache beneath the calm when he said 'stepfather'.

'Were you married?' She wanted him to say 'no' so badly it made her teeth hurt and she felt a mix of guilt and shame, but mostly relief when he shook his head, his expression bleak.

'When Jessie found out she was pregnant, I think she thought we'd get married, but I didn't want to do that. Not at first.'

His hands were clenching beneath hers, the whites of his knuckles visible through her open fingers.

'But you did want to marry her later?'

She phrased it as a question because again she wanted him to say no, but instead he nodded, and she felt that jerk of his head skewer her heart. 'I didn't love her. But I wanted to give her security. To prove that I could commit. But it was too late. She'd already left the country and gone home.'

His mouth curved into a smile that made her eyes burn.

'Maybe she would have stayed in the States if I'd

stepped up immediately like I should have done. But I didn't. So, she left and I never saw her again. Never talked to her again.'

There was a harshness to his voice now, an anger that she knew was preferable to pain. 'I'm sorry,' she said softly. Beneath her palms, his hands tightened a fraction.

'How did you meet her?'

'She was trying to parallel park her car and she reversed into mine. I'm not sure that she would ever have talked to me otherwise. I was eighteen when we met, and she was older than me. Twenty-two, I think. She didn't do any damage, but she took my number anyway. I didn't think she'd call but she did, and she was easy to talk to and cool about stuff that the girls my age weren't.'

She felt a pang of jealousy. 'You mean sex?'

He nodded slowly. 'Yeah. That was pretty much the sum of it. I mean, I liked her, but it was the summer before I went to college. I didn't want anything that serious. I never did, and she didn't either. But then she got pregnant.'

'And you're sure that—'

'She's mine?' He finished the end of her sentence for her. 'I did a paternity test. That's when Jessie talked about getting married. She arranged a scan, but I didn't go. I couldn't. I mean, I knew it was my baby except I didn't really believe it, and I think I knew that seeing it on screen would make it impossible to deny,' he said hoarsely. She thought back to the scan on St Martin and the way Harris had gripped her hand with emotion churning in his eyes.

'And you wanted to deny it?'

She thought of her own baby, slipping from its moorings like a beautiful gemstone disappearing into a crack between the floorboards.

He nodded again. 'Yes. I just wanted it all to go away. And then it did. Jessie left and I got what I thought I wanted.' His voice was flattened of emotion, which only seemed to emphasise the misery burning in his grey eyes. 'I went off to college and I told myself that I'd had a lucky escape. Because I knew, you see, that I couldn't be a husband or a father.'

'Why not?'

'You know why. You told me. Some people just aren't cut out for those kinds of commitments. You have to have luck or good judgement or both. My parents didn't have either of those things. They met at college, got drunk and had sex at some party and she got pregnant. They had nothing in common. Not even me.'

He stared past her at the moonlit water.

'They never said so, but I think I always knew that I'd messed up the lives they'd had planned. My mum was going to be a lawyer, but the pregnancy was really hard on her, and she had to drop out of college. They got married but I honestly can't remember them ever being happy. She was quietly angry all the time and my dad was in the navy flying jets when I was really small, so he was away quite a bit. And then he became an astronaut, and he wasn't even on the planet.'

'Why would you think that choosing a dark, lifeless vacuum over everything on Earth would be a dream of mine?' he'd asked her in the limo after they'd left the school, and she could still hear the anger in his voice. But now she could hear the pain layered beneath it. Understand it too.

'I was so lonely growing up,' he said then, and the stark honesty of his words caught her off balance. 'My family wasn't obviously damaged from the outside, so nobody really understood what it was like for me at home.'

'And you didn't want them to know anyway,' she said quietly.

His eyes found hers. 'No, I didn't. I guess I felt ashamed. Like it was my fault that they were together and so unhappy. And that's what I thought about when Jessie told me she was pregnant. The unhappiness and the loneliness. I couldn't see past it, couldn't see past the similarities between my parents' situation with me and my situation with Jessie and the baby and I panicked.'

'You were only eighteen, Harris, of course you panicked.'

'I know it must sound crazy, but I was so desperate not to repeat my parents' mistakes.'

It didn't sound crazy to her. She had spent years chasing after a life that had eluded generations of the women in her family solely to prove that she was different from them. And like Harris she had gone and repeated exactly the same mistakes.

Except being pregnant with his child didn't feel like a mistake. It felt like the most wonderful prize.

'I did nothing. I just acted like it wasn't anything to do with me. Only as soon as I got to college, all I could think about was Jessie and the baby, so I called her, but she didn't pick up. And I left messages, but she didn't reply and then her number changed so I came home from college and went to her apartment. That's when I found out she'd left the country almost straight after the scan.'

He tilted his head, gazing back up at the stars. 'Her flatmate told me. She'd given Jessie a lift to the airport. All she knew was that Jessie was going back to Australia for good. And then when I was walking out to the car, she ran after me. Said she'd forgotten to give me something. That Jessie had left it for me. She handed me an envelope and inside it was a photo. From the scan. The one I didn't go to.'

His mouth twisted into a shape that made something cold and serrated slice through her.

'There wasn't anything I could do. She was gone. I went back to college and that's when I met Tiger. Right from the start there was this rivalry between us but also an understanding that we both wanted the same things. It made me work hard and that was good because I didn't have time to think about Jessie or the baby.'

He hesitated then, and breathed in sharply as though he needed more air to say what he had to say next.

'And then about seven months later, out of the blue, she sent me a photo of the baby just after she was born and that's when I realised what I'd done. What I'd given up. Who I'd given up. My daughter. Jasmine.'

Eden remembered her own devastation when Liam had sent her the photo of his child. How she hadn't been able to eat, to sleep, to even get out of bed for days. She'd been dehydrated, her head had felt as if it were splitting in two, but that was nothing compared to the agony in her heart.

'Did she want to get back with you?'

He shook his head. 'No. She'd already met Eric by then.'

The name sounded painful in his mouth, as if just

saying it was giving him ulcers. 'I guess she thought I had a right to see the daughter I'd abandoned.' His hands tightened again so that she could almost picture the nails puncturing the skin on his palms. 'I think I had some kind of panic attack. I couldn't breathe, I felt like I was going to throw up and I wanted to talk to someone—'

Fragments of an earlier conversation vibrated through her body and suddenly it all made sense. That random act of aggression from a man who was strong and domineering and passionate but never violent. She hadn't understood it before but now she knew why it had happened.

'Tiger. You wanted to talk to Tiger. That's when you saw him with your girlfriend.'

He nodded slowly.

'What did you do?'

'Apart from punching him, you mean. Nothing. I wanted to do something, I guess I tried but there was nothing much to go on. All I knew was Jessie's name and that she'd worked in a bar in town.'

He shivered.

'I tried to find her for years. I even saved up some money and flew out to Australia, but it was only when the business took off that I was able to hire a private detective to look for her.'

'And you found her. And Jasmine.'

'It doesn't change anything.' He sounded exhausted and she knew without him even having to say so that, while this might be the first time he'd had this conversation with another person, he'd had it many times inside his head. 'Jasmine is settled now. She has a life. A father.'

'You're her father,' she said gently.

'Biologically maybe, but there's more to being a father than just getting someone pregnant.'

'There is. But parenting doesn't have a sell-by date. You still have time to be a dad to Jasmine. I know because I never spoke to my father until I was older than she is now.'

'He wasn't in your life at all?'

She shook her head. 'He didn't hang around when he found out my mum was pregnant with me. But then he turned up one day at the coffee shop where I worked after school. My mum had told him where to find me. I was so furious with her. And then he said he just wanted to talk and I lost it.'

In the event, she had done all the talking in a short, blistering monologue.

'I told him where to go. But he didn't give up. He sent me birthday cards and Christmas presents and postcards, and when I split with Liam and lost the baby he was the person I called. Not because I don't love my mum or my gran. But my dad has different strengths. He can put his own feelings to one side and that's what I needed. He made it bearable even though he didn't know what had happened. He was there for me, and one day you'll be there for Jasmine, and you will matter to her as much as she matters to you.'

Harris's eyes fluttered shut just for a few seconds, as if the possibility of that being true was too painful to look at head-on.

'What if Jessie doesn't want me in her daughter's life?'

'She doesn't have that choice. Any more than my mum did, because one day Jasmine is going to want to know who you are. But if Jessie's anything like my mum she'll want you to be in Jasmine's life. Because there's room for you in her life, and in her heart.'

The stars above blurred and there was a roaring in her ears that sounded like the sea. He wouldn't be in just Jasmine's heart, she realised, her stomach twisting with something that felt like pain only there was a sweetness beneath the sting.

Harris was in her heart too because she loved him. That was why she had gone looking for him, and probably in all honesty why she had agreed to come with him to St Barth's. Yet it was terrifying. Too terrifying to even think, much less admit to the man sitting in front of her. The man who had become as necessary to her as the moon was to the ocean.

'You're a good person, Eden,' he said quietly.

'So are you. But most importantly you're you. And the mistakes you make will be yours. Not your parents'. It's the same for me.' Only she hadn't realised that before. After Liam, she had simply assumed that she was fated to tread in her mother's and grandmother's footsteps. But there was no curse. She was her own person, and most women had a Liam in their life, especially when they were young.

She thought back to Harris flying her to the scan in his helicopter. It was true that he had wanted to check the baby was okay, but he had also wanted to take care of her. To make her feel safe and certain, and she did feel certain now, and not just about the baby. She felt confident in her judgement too.

'Both of us need to remember that, and if we do that and we keep talking then things will work out.' She gave him a small, swift smile. 'We're a good team.'

She had been going to say partnership but that had 'couply' overtones. Team was a business word that she could say without revealing the hope in her heart.

'We are.' He held her gaze, and she saw surprise and acknowledgement and something else she didn't recognise in his dark grey eyes.

'Although I probably deserve most of the credit,' she said, making a joke to cover up the way she was feeling. The way he made her feel.

'I've never met anyone like you.' His eyes were fixed on her face, and she felt something hot and liquid and electric skate across her skin as he reached up to brush his thumb across her cheek.

When he let his hand drop, she almost cried out in disappointment but instead she said quickly, 'We should probably get back.'

Her disappointment multiplied exponentially as he nodded, but then he reached out and caught her arm, his warm fingers curling round her wrist, and the sound of the waves seemed to swell and double in volume, or maybe that was the beat of her blood.

'Eden,' he said softly, stretching out the first syllable as if he never wanted to finish saying her name, and then he pulled her forward, his grip firm even though his hands were trembling slightly, and he fitted his mouth to hers.

His mouth was gentle and yet she could tell how much he needed to kiss her, and she breathed him in, tasting him, her love mingling with her hunger in what had to be the most delicious, intoxicating cocktail ever invented.

She moved his hand to her waist. Her breath was hot against his mouth as his fingers moved over her bare skin in tiny concentric circles, and she had no idea how something so light and imprecise could feel so good. Now they moved up to cup her breasts then back to her waist, making her skin tingle with a pleasure that she knew he was feeling too. He was taking his time, and she knew that this was about more than sex and bodies and that feverish need they had felt before. It was about closeness and two hearts beating the same rhythm, merging into one.

'I want you so badly,' he whispered.

'I want you too.' She buried her face against his throat, breathing in his scent. She could feel his pulse twitching against her cheek and then his fingers pulled at the string on her bikini, sliding over her thigh to where she was already soft and swollen.

'Then tell me what you want from me.'

The roughness in his voice sent a charge of electricity down her spine that she felt everywhere, and she was suddenly so ready for him. She wriggled forward, clumsy, and uncaring of her clumsiness, pressing her body against the hard, straining shape of his erection.

'I want this,' she gasped.

'Then take it. Take everything. I'm yours.'

His knuckles brushed against her labia just once, but it was enough and she pushed down the waistband of his swim shorts, freeing him into her hot hand and then guiding herself down onto him.

She moaned softly as she pushed against him. Her muscles clenched, and she started to shake with a pleasure that had no equal, and then seconds later Harris angled his hips and thrust up inside her, shuddering until finally he stilled against her. And they stayed like that for a long time, mindless and unravelled, clinging to one another beneath the moonlight.

The next day, their final day on the island, they both woke early for the first time in days. They made love slowly, taking their time, changing positions, their pleasure rising and tumbling them over like the waves outside their bedroom window. But his need for her never changed tempo and he found that thrilling and terrifying in equal measure.

'What time are we leaving to go back to New York?'

Harris glanced over to where Eden sat in one of his shirts that she'd somehow appropriated as her own.

'Whenever you want,' he said, leaning across the mattress to pour out some juice. He handed her a glass.

'Whenever I want? I thought the appointment for the paternity test was first thing tomorrow morning.' She gave him one of those teasing smiles that showed her small white teeth.

'It is. But we have a certain amount of flexibility, so you choose.'

She bit into her lip, and he felt a flicker of envy because her lips, her mouth, her body felt as if they belonged to him. 'Aren't you the boss?'

'I'm into power sharing at the moment,' he said, more to see her reaction than because he meant it. But maybe it was true, he thought, a moment later. With her, he was happy to give up control. Sometimes. *Under the right circumstances*, he thought, replaying the moment when she had straddled him on the beach.

Was it happiness he was feeling? He'd felt triumphant before when he'd won a big contract and obviously there was that calm that followed sex, although he'd never felt as sated as he did with Eden. But this feeling wasn't so much to do with sex. It was about wholeness and certainty—or at least that was the closest he could come to describing it.

And it was because of her. She'd made him feel whole and certain and lighter today than he had for years, and hopeful in a way that he had never felt before. But then a burden had been lifted from his shoulders. By Eden.

He had felt that he'd given up any right to being in Jasmine's life before she was born and that had felt unalterable. But Eden's relationship with her father had given a kind of shape to how that might change. He hadn't lost his daughter, just lost his way at the start of the journey to being her father. And no matter how many diversions or obstacles he met enroute, he wasn't going to give up the chance to find his place in his daughter's heart.

But he also wasn't ready yet to stop this thing with Eden.

Her eyes held his for a long beat of silence and his pulse twitched as she sat back on her haunches and began to unbutton her shirt, because of course she knew what he was thinking, and what he wanted.

'Then let's go this evening.'

They spent the rest of the day moving easily between the bedroom, the pool and the beach.

It felt natural, this rhythm between them. Domestic almost, except this was a holiday and like all holidays it had little to do with real life.

And when they got back to real life in New York, what then?

Leaving the city, he'd been entirely focused on not letting her out of his sight until he could do a paternity test. Arriving in the Caribbean, he'd had a different question spinning inside his head. What if I'm the father, what then? This was the more nuanced version of that because he had, privately at least, accepted that Eden was carrying his baby so there was no longer a 'what if'.

Which meant that their lives were going to be intertwined. But how?

On the flight back to New York they talked through how he could get back in touch with Jessie, and he realised once again how much he valued Eden's opinion. And that he had got used to having her around.

'Excuse me, Mr Carver, Ms Fennell.' John, the air steward, was smiling down at him. 'The pilot asked me to tell you that we'll be touching down in New York in around twenty minutes so if you could buckle up, please.'

'I was thinking we can drop by your apartment and pick up whatever you need and then go back to mine.'

Eden glanced over at him, her green eyes widening a fraction. 'We don't need to do that. I can just wing it until tomorrow morning.'

'You're right. You don't need to worry about any of that. If you give me the keys, I can get someone to pack up your things—'

'Pack them up?' He saw her jolt of surprise, but he was distracted by the light flush of colour along the curve of her cheeks and that sprinkling of freckles that came from spending a week in the sun. She had never looked more beautiful and, impulsively, he leaned forward and kissed her, his body hardening as he felt her mouth soften. There was a bedroom at the other end of the cabin. Could they—

'There's not enough time,' she whispered against his mouth.

He groaned. 'I could be quick—'

She gazed up at him. 'You don't need to be if I'm moving in with you. That is what you just suggested, isn't it?'

He nodded slowly, his need for her woven in with a relief that she seemed on board with that.

'It makes sense,' he said casually, his hand moving to caress her face.

Her eyes stayed steady on his but there was something vulnerable about her mouth. 'What do you mean?'

What did he mean? In truth, he didn't have a clear explanation, just that it felt like the right decision.

He shrugged. 'Like you said back at the villa, we're a good team. We like each other and the sex is incredible. I think we work.'

'But I don't work for you anymore, Harris,' she said slowly.

He frowned. 'That's not what I said, or what I meant.'

She stared at him, her face unreadable, but he could see the tightness around her eyes. 'No, you said that we like each other and that the sex is incredible.'

'I did. It is,' he said, her coolness kicking up sparks inside him. 'Why is that a bad thing?'

'It's not, it's just that it's not really—'

Not really enough, Eden thought, her stomach tensing around something hard and cold and unyielding.

Harris was frowning, his handsome face defying logic

and expectation to somehow look even more handsome. 'It's not what?'

'It's just not what I expected to happen,' she said at last.

His frown darkened. 'What did you expect? That you would just go back to your old life? We need to make this work. For our child's sake. That's what's important, and I know you agree.'

She did. She knew what it felt like to grow up conscious always of the absence of her father but cohabiting with someone who only 'liked' you would be a different kind of absence.

An absence of love.

Back on the island, it had been easy to tell herself that love was not a word to be used lightly. Better to let Harris give a name to what he was feeling than force it on him, because she was certain that his feelings matched hers. He was simply a few steps behind, but he would catch up eventually, take her hand and pull her close just as he always did.

She wanted to ask him if that was true, but she also wasn't quite ready for him to answer.

She cleared her throat. 'I do want to make this work. But we can't just go into this blind—'

'We're not,' he said calmly. 'We worked together for weeks.'

'Worked, not lived together.'

'We just spent a week doing that.'

'That wasn't real.' She shook her head because she wanted, no, needed him to protest, and he did.

'Not real. How wasn't it real? We ate together. We slept together. We talked, we laughed, we had fun…'

It was fun, the most fun she'd ever had in her life and yet with anyone else it would have felt mundane. But it had felt miraculous and extraordinary and beautiful when she'd caught Harris watching her as she put on her make-up or when he reached out to brush sand off her ankle or as he stole a kiss when the security detail had glanced away to glower at a yacht that was too close to the shoreline and she'd forgotten where she was, and how to breathe, and even her own name.

And yet, it also wasn't real, she realised, the chill in her stomach spreading.

'Yes, because we were on vacation.'

His face shifted, and she felt a pang of guilt. She was being unfair, but something had shifted between them; there was an awkward pragmatism that hadn't been there at the villa.

'I didn't realise that's how you felt.' He was staring past her, his grey eyes impenetrable. 'But yes, I suppose that is what it was. Only we're not on vacation anymore. You are still pregnant though. And if that is my baby you're carrying then I don't want to be cut out of his or her life.'

'You won't be. But living together—'

'Will mean that doesn't happen,' he cut across her, his voice not the voice of the man who'd whispered her name as he'd lifted her onto his big body or the man who had wrapped her in his arms and comforted her. Instead, he sounded like the impatient, autocratic CEO who had turned up unannounced at her apartment and steamrollered her into coming with him to St Barth's. Her wishes, her needs had been secondary to his.

Subservient, in fact. And now?

She shivered. Maybe they still were.

'So, you want us to act like a couple. That's your so-lution. To lie to our child. You want to pretend that we love each other.' And it would be a lie on his part, she realised as his expression shuttered. Whatever it had felt like at the time, that closeness, that feeling of being con-nected was just a hoax, a shimmering mirage beneath the Caribbean sun.

'I think it's unhelpful to frame it in those terms.' He sounded as if he were reading from a script. 'What we'll be doing is finding common ground and using it to act for the greater good.'

The greater good.

In other words, she was just a cog in a machine. Her moving in had nothing to do with her needs. It was about creating or simulating a family dynamic. She would be his partner but not really, just like with Liam, only then she had been ignorant of the deceit. This time she would be complicit.

'And what about me? Where do I fit into this?' Her voice trailed off as he met her gaze.

'You're the baby's mother.'

Her throat tightened so that it was hard to speak, but she had to know, had to ask, 'And if I wasn't pregnant?'

In the heavy silence that followed her question she felt her heart, her stupid hope-filled heart, split in two and she stared at him, staggered by how much silence could hurt.

There was a bump as the plane's wheels hit the runway and she was glad because it gave her an excuse to grip the armrest as she tried to breathe through the crushing pain in her chest.

'We can—'

She shook her head. 'There is no we, Harris. And I won't be moving into your apartment. I need my own space.'

'I don't understand. I'm offering you security and stability. A life that most people dream of.'

'And that's very generous but I don't just want those things.'

'What else is there?'

Love, she thought. Reciprocal, equal, eternal.

But love wasn't on offer here. It never had been.

'There's love,' she said, lifting her eyes to meet his. 'You see, I like you as much as you like me, Harris. You know I do, but what you don't know is that I also love you. And I know you're scared of loving someone. I know because I'm scared too, so scared that after Liam I made a promise never to let myself get that close to anyone. But I couldn't not get close to you because you're here…' she tapped her forehead '…and here.' Now she touched her stomach.

'But most of all, you're here.' She pressed her hand against her heart. 'At the villa, I thought there was a chance you might love me too—don't worry, I know you don't. But I want… I need to be loved, not just liked. And I don't want to be a team player or act for the greater good. I want to have a partner. Someone who wants me for who I am and not because I'm carrying their baby.'

She waited, hoping, yearning, but after an interminable moment he nodded slowly. 'I understand. And I'm sorry.'

Then he was reaching down and unbuckling his belt and he was on his feet and moving up the cabin to talk to the pilot. She stared after him, mute with misery, wondering how it was possible that in the space of a moment she had gone from talking about moving in together to falling into this deep and lightless abyss from which there was no escape.

Later she would wonder how she'd got off the plane. She had no memory of the car journey back to her apartment.

When the limo stopped, he got out of the car without a word, and she had no option but to stand beside him in an awkward silence that was almost as crushing as the sudden distance between them.

'Thank you for taking me to the villa. Could you text me the clinic's address and the appointment time for the test and I'll meet you there?' she added quickly because she'd had enough of this brutal, new version of their relationship.

'I can pick you up.'

'There's no need.' She turned quickly because it hurt too much to keep looking at him but as she began to walk away, she felt his fingers catch her wrist and she turned towards him, hope spiralling up inside her.

'Eden.' He was looking straight ahead but his hand tightened a fraction, and she heard the sudden hoarseness in his voice like a reprieve. It was going to be okay. He was going to admit that he'd spoken hastily, that he'd not understood what he was feeling. That he loved her and wanted her in his life because he couldn't live without her.

'I've got a conference call first thing, so I'll make my own way there, but I'll send a car for you. Please take it.'

His voice was calm and detached, as if their conversation on the plane had never taken place. As if nothing had ever happened between them. He leaned in and brushed her cheek lightly with his lips and then he let go of her wrist and walked over to the limo. She watched it drive away just as her mother had watched all those other cars back in San Antonio and as it disappeared round the corner, the wave of misery and despair that was rising inside her toppled over, swallowing her whole.

CHAPTER TEN

SIDESTEPPING SMOOTHLY PAST a group of people gazing at a young man and woman playing covers of eighties hits on their guitars, Harris took the incline at a run, closely followed by his security detail.

He was running on the loop around Central Park. Mostly he ran before breakfast. Sometimes he ran this late but not on the street and not when he'd just stepped off a plane.

Jonas, his head of Security, hadn't said a word when he'd appeared in running gear and told him that he wanted to head out for a jog, but no doubt he was thinking that his boss could just as easily have gone and pounded on the running machine in his gym. Except that would mean staying at the apartment and he couldn't do that right now. Couldn't be alone in those beautiful, cavernous rooms.

Their emptiness haunted him.

She haunted him.

Eden.

She had been his paradise, but now he was cast out in the darkness, and it was all his fault.

His foot slid on a stone, and he stumbled.

'I'm okay.' He held up his hand as his security men swarmed forward.

He didn't want to stop, not yet. If he stopped, he would start replaying that conversation on the plane and he didn't want to have to hear the stupid, insensitive and inaccurate words that had come out of his mouth. All that nonsense about finding common ground and using it to act for the greater good.

The greater good.

His jaw tightened. What a sanctimonious coward.

No wonder he was alone. Each time someone tried to get close to him, he pushed them away. Jessie. Tiger. Eden.

He had let her leave, no, he had driven her to her doorstep, even though she had opened herself up, made herself vulnerable. She had told him the truth and offered her love. She had been honest and brave, but he was too scared to go beyond offering her stability and the trappings of wealth.

As he passed another of the entrances to the park, his body turned as it had done each time he was given the chance to leave. It would be so easy to let his legs take him where he wanted to go. To Eden's apartment.

It was tempting to do just that, because he missed her so badly that his bones ached.

But there was no point. He had made her feel that she was unimportant to him when the opposite was true and anything he said now would sound forced and fabricated. He had messed up everything, again. Made as many mistakes as he had all those years ago, only this was worse because at some point Eden would find the love she was looking for, and then he would have to endure watching her raise their child with another man.

Only it wasn't just about that. It never had been, but he hadn't realised it until now.

It was about Eden. Her smile, her strength, her intelligence, her bravery. And how she made him feel. Strong and certain. And seen and heard.

If only he could prove that to her, but there was no combination of words that would offer such a simple solution.

Yet sometimes actions spoke louder than words, he thought, his legs slowing down to a steady jog.

'Is everything all right, Mr Carver?'

He turned towards where his head of Security was jogging alongside him. 'It will be, Jonas. Call Owen, tell him we'll be home in ten minutes. I need him ready and waiting.' He knew from the expression on Jonas' face that the panic punching him in the stomach must be audible in his voice, but he didn't care. All he cared about was seeing Eden again. And getting her to give him a second chance. To give them a chance.

After the open skies and glittering seas of the Caribbean, the city felt crowded and noisy, and Eden was glad that she was sitting in the limo Harris had sent. She had dithered about taking it, but despite having fallen into a coma-like sleep last night, she still felt exhausted this morning. Too exhausted to make a stand.

She gazed through the glass at the people walking to work. What exactly was she taking a stand against anyway? Not taking his limo wasn't going to make Harris love her.

Nothing was going to do that.

She hadn't allowed herself to think about that awful conversation on the plane. Maybe she never would. Her one consolation was that Harris would never bring it up. No doubt, he would keep everything polite and formal.

Thinking that made her want to cry and she must have made some kind of noise because she saw the driver glance up at his rear-view mirror.

'Don't worry, Ms Fennell, we won't have any more hold-ups. I'll get you there on time.'

She smiled stiffly. On the flight out to St Barth's, this appointment had felt like the moment she would get her life back, or at least her freedom. But now freedom just meant a lifetime of being the mother of his child. Not the woman he loved or wanted or needed.

The clinic looked more like a boutique hotel than a medical centre. Even the staff looked as if they'd stepped off a catwalk. She sat and waited in a lounge area with expensive leather armchairs and tried to brace herself for the moment when she saw him again. If only she had thought to practise her expression in the mirror.

But had she done so it would have been a waste of time because he didn't turn up.

The doctor called her into the office and offered her a seat. Smiling apologetically, she told her that Mr Harris's people had called to let her know that he was unable to attend.

'I see.' In other words, he had thought about it and decided to take her claim of wanting space literally. Or maybe he was proving a point.

Reaching down, she began pushing up the sleeve of her blouse. 'I assume I can still do the blood sample.'

Now the doctor frowned. 'That won't be necessary.'

'Do we have to do it together, then?' Eden stared at her in confusion. 'Surely that isn't necessary.'

'It isn't, but that's not why I'm not going to take your blood,' the doctor said gently. 'Mr Carver has cancelled the paternity test.'

She nodded. 'Because he was unable to make the appointment? Did he say when he wanted to rebook it?'

The doctor cleared her throat. 'He doesn't. Apparently, it's not necessary anymore.'

The room seemed to sway a little. Not necessary. Like her.

She had no idea how she left the clinic. The black limo was hovering by the kerb, and it took every ounce of strength she had to compose her face into a careless smile and get in.

Call him, she told herself. Confront him. Ask him why he doesn't want to do a test. But even thinking about hearing his voice made her feel queasy.

What was the point of asking him something when she already knew the answer? Which was that he had backed off. Probably she had scared him off with her talk of love. And she couldn't face another of those awful, lopsided conversations that made the floor feel as if it were undulating beneath her feet.

Either way, she had got her wish, she thought as she walked back into the apartment. She had all the space she wanted.

And time on her hands too.

What with the pregnancy and then going to St Barth's, she hadn't booked in another client but, right now, she didn't need the money.

She needed to think about this baby and the life she was going to give him or her. Harris might have backed off but that didn't mean her life had to end. She wasn't going to shut down as she had after Liam. She was a different person now. Not just older, and wiser. She knew who she was, and she was proud of herself and everything she had achieved.

And she was going to keep achieving, keep moving forward in her life. She would even include Harris if that was what he wanted. She wasn't going to cut him out of his child's life, but their interactions would be on her terms, not his.

For now, though, she was, if not happy, then content to potter around the apartment. She would buy a bunch of pregnancy books and get prepared and in the meantime she was going to watch every possible vampire drama she could stream. She had lunch, then went out to buy some plants, but that was all she did for the rest of the day except call her mom and grandma and her dad and tell them that she was pregnant. They were all so supportive, and knowing that she was loved and supported unconditionally in her choices helped slightly mitigate the sadness she felt about her baby's father disappearing off the face of the earth.

Was that why she had agreed to going on this stargazing walk? So that she could scan the night skies for the man who had first shown them to her?

It was her neighbour who had invited her when they'd met on the stairs. Professor Paige Geffen was an archetypal boffin, with her wild grey curls and open-toed sandals, who lectured on astrophysics at various universities around the world, including Columbia University. And when she was back in New York, she ran a monthly walk to Pier 45 on the Hudson River.

They were not a big crowd, but everyone was very friendly and excited, and she was pleased she had gone. With Liam, she had stopped doing things that reminded her of him, but she wasn't going to do that this time. Why should she limit her life like that? Anyway, it was something she and Harris had shared, and she wanted to be able to share that with the baby too.

She had been spoiled, she realised as she gazed up at the sky. It wasn't as clear here as it had been from Harris's office, and certainly not as clear as the sky in St Barth's. But she could still spot various constellations.

'Now, can anyone tell me which is the brightest light in the sky?' Paige was asking.

'Is it Orion's belt?' someone suggested.

'No, that's a good answer, but not the right one.'

'It's the space station.'

Eden felt her heart flip over. She spun round, her eyes seeking out the owner of the deep, husky voice.

Harris. Lounging against the wooden railings, looking just as he had when she'd walked into that bar. Dark jeans, leather jacket and that beautiful, sculpted face, grey eyes fixed on her face intently as if she were his Pole Star.

As the stargazers moved further down the pier, she stood frozen to the spot as he detached himself from the railing and walked over to her slowly. Even though it twisted her insides, she couldn't drag her gaze away and, stupid though it was, it was still a joy to see him, despite the pain.

He stopped in front of her, and she stared up at him feeling slightly delirious.

'Stubble,' she said hoarsely.

He frowned. 'What?' Then he touched his jaw. 'Yes, I haven't shaved today.'

It suited him, but so would a bin bag. She should have walked away as soon as she saw him, she realised. Even a couple of feet was too close for comfort. She could already feel her body responding to his…

She cleared her throat. 'Why not?'

'I guess I forgot.'

'Is that why you missed the paternity test? Did you forget that too?'

'No, that was for a different reason,' he said and there was an ache in his voice that made her want to step forward and comfort him, but he wasn't hers to comfort, she reminded herself.

'So why are you here now?' She took a step back. 'How did you know where I was? Are you having me followed?'

That hurt, more than it should. That he didn't love her was a blow, but that he didn't trust her was crushing.

'No, I went to your apartment, and you didn't answer when I rang so I buzzed the supervisor. He told me where you were.'

'You still haven't told me why you're here,' she said flatly, because she knew why. 'Let me guess, you want to rebook the paternity test.' She shook her head, remembering the shock of his absence, the carelessness of his second-hand apology. 'Do you know what it felt like being told by the doctor that you'd cancelled it?

You didn't even have the manners to call me or leave
a message.'

He took a step forward and she saw that, beneath the
stubble, he looked pale and there were dark smudges
under his eyes. Once again, she had the stupid, self-
harming urge to put her arms around him. *Not mine to
hold*, she told herself.

'I know.' He looked wretched, as wretched as when
he'd told her about Jasmine. But Jasmine was his daughter, and she was just the mother of his child.

'And I'm sorry.' He breathed out unsteadily. 'I wanted
to call you. I wanted to see you, not to tell you about the
test but because I missed you so much. But I knew that I
was being selfish, that I was only doing it for myself and
that if I saw you or spoke to you, I'd hurt you.'

'You did hurt me.' Her voice cut across the silent pier,
and she felt the stargazers' eyes move towards her in
unison.

'I know,' he said again. 'And I hate that I did that. I
hate that I was such a coward.'

'Well, I hate you.'

He ran a hand over his face. 'Is that true?' His voice
shook a little as he spoke. 'I mean, I'd understand if you
did.'

She was shaking her head. 'This isn't fair of you, Harris, turning up like this, making me feel things I don't
want to feel—'

'But I want you to feel them, because I feel them too.'

Considering everything that had happened, she had
thought she was doing well. Yes, she had thought about
him. Worried about him. Wondered where he was and

what he was doing, but she hadn't spent every second weeping or raging. But now she wanted to do both.

'Don't do that. Don't say things you don't mean.'

'I do mean them.' There were shadows as well as stubble on his face. He looked exhausted and heartbreakingly beautiful, but her heart didn't need to be broken any more.

'And why would I believe you?'

'Because I can't lie to you, Eden. I can lie to everyone else—I have lied. And I can even lie to myself, but I can't lie to you. It breaks me,' he said hoarsely.

'You said I was just the mother of your baby.'

'I did, but then I got back to the apartment, and I hated it. I hated you not being there, and I hated that I cared but I couldn't stop myself, so I went out for a run in Central Park. I kept wanting to run to your apartment and tell you that I was wrong, and that I loved you, but I was scared that you'd take me back. I kept thinking about all the people I'd pushed away and all the times I'd been pushed away and I got scared that I didn't know how to love and that I'd hurt you even more than I already had, and I never want to hurt you.'

His grey eyes were fierce and brighter than any star. 'And then I realised that there weren't any words that could prove that I love you. That I needed to show you instead, and that's why I didn't turn up for the paternity test. Because I don't need proof that I'm our baby's father. I love you and I will love our baby, and I want the three of us to be a family. So, can we do that, Eden? Can we be a family? Will you let me take care of you? Both of you?'

Eden stared at him, her pulse slowing to a heavy thud,

her heart spilling over with a love that was equalled if not surpassed by the love in Harris's voice and in his eyes.

'I'd like that. I'd like that a lot,' she whispered. And finally she reached for him.

Sucking in a breath that was spiked with relief, Harris pulled her against his heaving chest, curving his body around hers so that their foreheads were touching. Moments earlier he had felt as though he had been fighting for his life. And he had been, because Eden was his sunlight and his oxygen.

Only now she was looking up at him with those beautiful soft green eyes that made him feel so seen and clutching at him as if she never wanted to let him go.

'I am still scared,' he said then, because he couldn't lie to her. But she didn't pull away. She just pulled him closer, close enough that he could feel her heart beating in time to his.

'I'm scared too, but we want to be with each other.'

'Yes. Yes.' He nodded, although it wasn't a question and she smiled.

'It's not going to be easy all the time, but we want to make it work, and we're a good team.' She reached up and took his hand and pressed it against her stomach.

'We're not a team, we're partners…' he brushed his lips against her mouth '…and lovers…' he kissed her softly '…and soulmates.' Then he deepened the kiss, parting her lips and kissing her hungrily, both lost and found in her embrace.

EPILOGUE

THE LIGHT WAS different this high up, Eden thought as she shifted her cheek against the pillow. In Harris' New York triplex, two hundred metres above the city, it was soft and miraculous. Like the way Harris was touching her.

He was beside her, his muscular body propped up on his forearm, his fingers travelling over her body as they always did with that same mix of reverence and compulsion. Tracing the swell of her breast. Caressing the curve of her hip and then moving to the slick heat between her thighs as she wanted him to.

The breath squeezed out of her body as his finger stilled against the pulse beating there. Always beating there, matching the pulse of her heart. Because he was here with her. The man she loved and who loved her, she thought, her stomach swooping as he pulled her towards him and kissed her greedily.

'Do we have time?' he mumbled against her mouth.

'Yes…'

It was just one word but it was loaded with longing and intent and as she watched his pupils widen, her need for him made it impossible to be still. She arched closer, the air punching out of her lungs as the blunt tip of his erection slid inside her and then he was pushing deeper until there was nowhere left to go, his hands shaping her to fit her around him as his breathing grew ragged. Just like the first time it was astonishing and incomparable and right, so very right, and she was nothing but heat and a shuddering, flickering pleasure that pulsed through her in wave after shattering wave.

Afterwards, he kissed her everywhere that he had touched, before pulling her close enough that she could feel his heartbeat overlapping hers.

He was hers now. Not just physically and emotionally but legally.

They had married a month after getting back from St Barth's. It was a small, quiet ceremony, because it suited them both. It was perfect in every detail from her simple white silk dress to the emotion in his voice as he'd made his vows in the presence of their parents. All four of them. In a room together. Plus her grandma, of course.

They had, all of them, looked a little stunned to be there. But happy too, and, as far as his parents went, grateful.

As they should be. Her fingers tightened around his shoulders, and she felt a fiercely protective rush of love and pride, remembering the shock of his beauty as he'd stood waiting for her at the front of the room.

He had looked as a bridegroom should. Tall, blond and so swooningly handsome in his dark suit that the registrar had kept getting distracted. It had felt like a dream as he'd taken her hand and squeezed it as if he, too, had needed to reassure himself that this was real, that she was real.

'What are you thinking about?'

She glanced up. Harris was gazing down at her, his

eyes fixed on her face, but his hand was moving again, following the contours of her belly.

'I was thinking about our wedding day. About how handsome you looked and how lucky I felt. How lucky I feel.' She could do this now. Speak without being afraid that she was giving too much away because nothing was held back. Letting him see how much she wanted and needed him was still terrifying but also intoxicating and necessary.

Reaching out, he cupped her cheek. 'I'm the lucky one.'

She felt his words, the truth of them, resonating through her and suddenly it was hard to do anything more than nod because she had thought this was something that happened to other people, other women. That for her it would always stay as some unattainable goal dancing just out of reach.

But there was an honesty and a straightforwardness to how they spoke to one another that she knew was as rare as it was beautiful.

'I love you,' she said softly.

His eyes held hers for a long beat. 'I know.' He did, but it was still new to him, and he liked to hear it and she liked to say it. Liked to watch his eyes soften—

A cry. Tiny but imperative.

Harris turned, they both did, their eyes arrowing onto the state-of-the-art baby monitor on the bedside table.

On the screen, the baby was moving, kicking up her feet and reaching her hands over her head, wispy golden curls framing her face, her green eyes bright in the soft morning light. She made another experimental cry like a kitten mewing, testing the sound, flexing her power and then, as if she was pleased with the results, her face split into a gummy smile that matched the one pulling at the corners of Eden's mouth.

Carina.

The look on Harris's face, so fierce and paternal, almost undid her.

Their daughter had been born nearly three weeks ago. The birth had been a long and exhausting process made worse by the panic that had risen unbidden and unwelcome when her water had suddenly broken. Her birth plan had been scrapped. The scented candles were left unlit. Her favourite songs stayed un-played. Nothing on her list made it to the hospital.

Except Harris, and that was all that mattered. He was all she'd needed.

And he had been there the entire time. Taking the baby from the midwife and laying her on Eden's stomach so that she could feel her daughter's heart beating, his tears mingling with hers as he'd murmured garbled words of love and joy into her ear.

A lot had happened in the run-up to their daughter's birth.

Aside from getting married, Harris had reached out to Tiger McIntyre and after talking on the phone they had met up with him and his wife, Sydney. It had been a nerve-racking encounter. Tiger was as toned and taut with nervous energy as Harris and for a moment, as they'd stared at each other warily, it had felt like a mistake. But then Sydney had grabbed Eden's hand and told her that they were going to be friends whatever happened between their husbands, and they had left them to it.

She had half expected to come back and find them

lying bloodied and spent on the floor of Tiger's open-plan living area that matched Harris's in scale and style. But when the two women had returned from a morning of mocktails and massage, both men had been sprawled on the sofas drinking beer and playing a first-person shooter as if they were back at college.

As for the drill bit: it turned out that there was no IP theft. As had happened so many times in the past, they had simply had the same inspiration.

'You know we talked about Tiger and Sydney being Carina's godparents?' she said, shifting closer to touch the marvel of his jaw. 'How do you feel about asking them today at lunch?'

Harris turned away from the monitor to look at his wife.

Eden. Having her in his life was like being in an earthly paradise. The tension that had hummed inside him for so long had vanished. His mind was mellow with pleasure right now but this, the two of them, was about so much more than sex. There was a quiet there now and yet he knew that he was heard and seen by Eden. He knew too that even when they were apart she was thinking about him. Thinking about when she would see him again, and the things she would ask him and tell him.

For each of them, that knowledge was a comfort and a necessity, a magnetic North that centred them. A pole star that combined the pull of the moon and the warmth of the sun.

But that was just the beginning. Eden had given him so much more. She had helped him start to create something approximating a relationship with his parents. And then there was Tiger.

In that moment of reconciliation, he'd felt both relief and gratitude to Eden and Sydney. Tiger had felt the same way, and now their friendship was a full-on bromance, much to the amusement of their wives.

He had no idea how Eden had made that happen. Just thinking about the man he'd been, the man he would have remained if they had never met, made him pull her close and hold her tight. Because he *was* lucky to have found her and he knew that she could not be replicated.

She was his equal. A partner and a muse because being with her seemed to stimulate his brain as much as his body so that his business was accelerating like a solar probe.

And then there was Carina.

His beautiful daughter. He had seen her every day of her life. She was a miracle. A blessing. And he loved being a hands-on father.

'I was thinking that might be a good time to ask them too.'

Eden kissed him lightly on the lips and he felt her smile ripple through him. 'We might even let them do a little bit of babysitting. Give Tiger some practice before Sydney has the baby. You can give him some tips.'

'I'm still learning.'

'You are. But you're a natural.'

Surprisingly, he was. But he got a kick out of hearing her say it. From knowing that she said it because she cared, because she knew that he still needed that reassurance sometimes.

Eden rolled onto him then, her eyes moving to check the monitor. But this time his gaze stayed put because she was straddling him now, and her breasts were there, fuller from the milk, and he felt his body stir.

'Hi, Carina.' The monitor again. This time, a child's voice with an Australian twang, then a giggle.

Eden leaned forward, laughing, and he groaned softly then grinned, a big, stupid grin. Because that was something else that he had to thank his wife for.

Jasmine was in his life too, now.

Reaching out to her mother had been a big step, but Eden had been by his side. Jessie had been cautious at first, understandably, but on Eden's advice he had let her set the pace and five months ago, Jasmine had come to visit him in New York with Jessie and her husband, Eric.

It had burned at first, hearing his daughter calling Eric Dad.

But now she called him Dad too. Which was fine because, as Eden had reminded him, two things could be true at once. And each time he saw his eldest daughter, he felt the connection deepen, not just with him but with Eden too, so that by the time Carina was born it was Jasmine who had chosen her baby sister's name, picking her favourite constellation in the night sky.

'Can I bring Carina in to you? Please. I'll be careful.' Jasmine was squinting hopefully up at the camera.

'Yes, just remember to support her head.'

'I know, Daddy.'

Watching Harris's face soften, Eden felt a deep, almost painful tug of happiness. Her love for him was so sharp, so compelling.

'I better put some clothes on,' she said softly, reaching for her robe.

'I guess you should.' He touched her cheek. 'I love you. I love this.'

'I love it too.' She pulled him closer and kissed him fiercely and for a moment there was just the warm touch of their lips and the press of their bodies and then Jasmine came into the room, carrying her baby sister, and just like that they were the family they had both longed to be for so long.

* * * * *

If Nine-Month Contract *left you wanting more,*
then be sure to check out the first installment in
the Ruthless Rivals duet
Boss's Plus-One Demand

And why not explore these other stories
from Louise Fuller?

Returning for His Ruthless Revenge
Her Diamond Deal with the CEO
One Forbidden Night in Paradise
Undone in the Billionaire's Castle
Reclaimed with a Ring

Available now!